W9-ATF-327

ALSO BY KATHRYN WORTH

New Worlds for Josie

They Loved
to
Laugh

by
Kathryn Worth

Illustrated by
Marguerite de Angeli

BETHLEHEM BOOKS · IGNATIUS PRESS
BATHGATE, N.D.   SAN FRANCISCO

Copyright © 1942 by Kathryn Worth Curry
Published by arrangement with Random House Children's Books,
a division of Random House, Inc.

All rights reserved

Cover art by Marguerite de Angeli
Cover design by Davin Carlson

First printing, September 1996

ISBN 978-1-883937-16-4
Library of Congress: 96-83480

Bethlehem Books • Ignatius Press
10194 Garfield Street South
Bathgate, ND 58216
www.bethlehembooks.com

Printed in the United States on acid free paper

Manufactured by Thomson-Shore, Dexter, MI (USA); RMA74JM40, August, 2015

Author's Note

I WISH TO EXPRESS indebtedness for the use of a few brief quotations, embedded in the text of this book, from the *Correspondence of Jonathan Worth*, edited by J.G. de Roulhac Hamilton and published by the North Carolina Historical Commission. I am indebted also to Mr. James Sprunt's *Chronicles of the Lower Cape Fear* for one short quotation.

My thanks for their reminiscences and loan of books and photographs go to the following gracious people: Mrs. Joshua Murrow, Miss Laura D. Worth, Mrs. Nellie Rowe Jones, Mrs. Mary Macy Marley, Mrs. Sallie Carson, Miss May McAlister, Mrs. Nellie Savery, and Mrs. Pearl Jennings. My debt to Alexander Worth McAlister, for his brilliant aid in securing historical and legendary lore, I can never repay.

To that branch of the family which, due to the laws of fiction, was required to be cut off from the ancestral tree, I express regret. My intent in this story is to re-create as nearly as possible the inward truth of historic character, not the outward accuracy of historic detail.

Table Of Contents

※※※※※※※※※※※※※※※※※※

To
My Quaker great-great-grandparents
EUNICE AND DAVID WORTH
of
Guilford County, North Carolina,
and to
that one of their living descendants named
ALEXANDER WORTH McALISTER

※※※※※※※※※※※※※※※※※※

THEY LOVED TO LAUGH

CHAPTER I

Over the Next Hill

"OVER THE NEXT HILL is the house, Martitia. Lift your eyes from your lap long enough to look ahead. You'll see the Gardner house in a minute."

"Yes, Doctor David." The girl in the gig lifted grave blue eyes to the man beside her on the seat. The motion of the two-wheeled cart stirred her long skirts. She folded tighter the small hands in her blue homespun lap. Then she stared ahead of her up the country road.

"Don't be afraid, child. Every last Gardner will welcome you from the bottom of his heart. You may find five big, tall boys frightening at first. But you'll soon get used to them. My wife Eunice and my daughter Ruth will see to that."

The pointed face of the girl quivered. "I'm not used to big boys. My father and mother never held any store by boys." Over the words "father" and "mother" the low voice faltered and broke.

Dr. David reached out a hand and patted the bonnet

that almost covered the dark hair. "Your father and your mother would not want you to keep so heavy a heart. They died with a good hope, and they gave you into my care for keeping. They expected that time would lighten the load of your grief. Time will do it, my child. Wait a while. Your father and your mother are at rest from their labors. Someday you will meet them again in another state of being. For their sakes you must learn to smile again."

Martitia tightened her soft lips. She brushed the tears away with an unconscious gesture. "I'll try, Doctor David."

Dr. David took his whip and pointed suddenly past the horse's back, up the road ahead. His handsome black eyes sparkled. "There's the Gardner house, child. See the roof yonder and the white fence about it? I picked the best spot for a house in Guilford County when I came here to North Carolina from Nantucket. That was 1800. Thirty-one years ago, come this Thanksgiving time, I first stood at the foot of this little slope as you're seeing it today and picked this land for my own. We Gardners were always good pickers. Good pickers of land and of women."

Martitia stared up the low slope at the sturdy house at the top. She saw the hipped roof, the big brick chimneys, the long sloping yard full of trees. Even the untrained eyes of a city-bred girl could tell that the red earth held its fertility well, for the trees in the yard showed strong in their growth.

Martitia's small bones ached from jostling over miles of rolling Piedmont uplands today. How many times had she and Dr. David splashed through the fords of shallow streams? Her voice was faint now when she spoke. "Will all your five sons be there to meet us at one time?"

The big man's roar of laughter rang out across the cornfields. "If I know Jonathan and Milton and Barzillai and Clarkson and Addison as well as I think I do, they'll be lying in wait at the gate of the fence to attack me like Indians or to throw a bushel of soft apples at me. That is, they will if they see me coming. And I guess they will. After six days of having things on the farm to themselves, those five boys will have enough deviltry stored up in them for twenty regiments. Their mother and their sister won't be able to stop them. They'll be rarin' to go. It's a good thing I'm home from Randolph County."

Martitia spoke gravely. "It must be a hard thing to be a doctor, and to go such a long way to help sick people."

"Doctors go where they're needed. Especially when there's typhoid in two counties at once, like there is now in Guilford and Randolph. My practice is always extensive. It's not uncommon for me to be called over in July like this from Centre to Asheborough. I'm glad to be home, though."

Dr. David paused in his talk. He drew the horse's head toward the open gate in the fence at the side of the road. His black eyes began to shine with suppressed mirth. "Not a sound from those five boys yet. This silence is powerful suspicious. Well, that's all right. I've got a surprise for those boys this time! They may have apples for me. But *I've* got a *girl* for them!"

Before the girl could answer something round whizzed crazily past her low shoulder. Dr. David reached out and dragged the small, startled figure down with him into the bottom of the gig. His big frame was shaking with laughter. "Duck those overripe apples," he said. "Those boys are going to pelt us now."

And suddenly all the air over the gig was full of flying apples. From everywhere and from nowhere they seemed to come in their hurtling flight. Martitia huddled against Dr. David in the bottom of the cart. The apples plopped and sang and zoomed above their heads. Once a big, soft globe struck Dr. David's arm where he had thrown it protectingly over Martitia's bent body. Dr. David shook with redoubled delight. Martitia could feel the pulp from the mellow apple spatter itself over her cheek. She cowered against Dr. David.

Then it was all over as rapidly as it had begun. Silence fell over the gig. The silence was broken by a volley of cries. Out of the wide-spreading branches of a tree near the gate dropped five whooping figures. If they had been five chimpanzees they could not have startled Martitia more. Yet Dr. David and the unimpressed horse seemed equally untroubled and unaware of anything out of the ordinary in this remarkable reception. Martitia straightened. She stared at the five whooping figures.

Dr. David climbed down from the gig. He stood, large and handsome and ruddily laughing, and helped Martitia to descend.

Five boys advanced out of the shadows of the trees into the late-afternoon light. To Martitia they all looked enormous. Knowing her own brief five feet of height, she could not be sure that they were as large as they seemed to her. But they all appeared as giants and of about the same size.

"Thought you had your old father in a bad corner that time, didn't you, sons?" chuckled Dr. David. "Well, I wasn't surprised by those bad apples a mite. The ones that are going to be surprised this time are you boys, not me. Mind your manners. I've brought home a visitor." He took Martitia's hand and drew her gently forward. "This is Miss Martitia Howland, of Virginia, lately of Asheborough."

Martitia shrank against Dr. David. The boys came forward one by one. From the lack of bewilderment in their faces, it appeared that this was no new scene to them, greeting unexpected visitors from Dr. David's gig.

"This is Jonathan, my eldest son." Dr. David spoke proudly.

Martitia peered up at Jonathan. She saw a tall young man with keen hazel eyes and a magnificent forehead. His slender nose was well formed. The mouth beneath it was wide and powerful. He said nothing, only looked down at her.

"Quiet he is, this Jonathan," chuckled Dr. David. "But he's got opinions."

Martitia put out her small fingers. They were enveloped in a grasp that made her wince.

"And this is Clarkson," Dr. David continued.

Martitia looked at the second boy in line. He had brilliant black eyes and black hair like his father. She found herself smiling at Clarkson in spite of her terror. Something in the curve of his beautifully shaped mouth drew forth her heart.

"And this is Milton."

Milton moved energetically forward. He twinkled down at Martitia with an irrepressible brown glance.

Then there were big, slow-moving Barzillai and young Addison with his unruly hair and large ears. Martitia watched them pass in a daze. She felt that hundreds of boys must be in this yard and that all of them were enormous and full of laughter.

She turned to Dr. David. "Are there any more of them? Is this all?"

The five boys and their father roared. Then there came a running of footsteps. A young girl appeared from the direction of the hip-roofed house. The boys laughed harder than ever.

"Here's another boy, Martitia. Only he's got on skirts. He's Ruth, our sister." Clarkson's was the voice that spoke.

Martitia was too dazed to register anything about the newly come girl except that she was nearly as tall as the boys and had large hands.

The five boys went away in a noisy bunch, leading Dr. David's horse and cart toward the barn at the back of the house. Ruth and Dr. David and Martitia approached the house and mounted the four stones that formed the steps to the inbuilt porch.

A little, compact, stocky woman came out on the porch from within. "Thee was a long time getting home from Randolph County, David. Thee has been gone from First Day to Sixth Day. How were the Friends in Asheborough?"

She caught sight of Martitia now in the waning July light. "Thee has brought us a visitor, David?" She put out both hands to Martitia. "Welcome, child. Thy face looks tired. A bit of good supper will set that to rights. My husband never knows when to stop his cart on long trips and get rest or nourishment. I'll reckon he has given thee no food since breakfast."

Dr. David looked abashed. "Truly spoken, Eunice. I

forgot the child needed food since we left Randolph County at breakfast time."

He turned to Martitia. "This is your aunt Eunice, child. Everybody in Guilford County calls my wife 'Aunt Eunice.' So be it with you too."

He gave Martitia into Eunice's welcoming arms. "I have brought you John and Lucy Howland's girl, Martitia. Martitia will bide with us here at Centre for a while."

"Thee is right welcome, Martitia. Come inside to supper."

No explanations asked, no questions! Martitia was bewildered. Just "thee is welcome, Martitia." Even in hospitable Richmond, Virginia, where she had been born and reared, the girl knew she had never seen welcome more gracious than this. And in neighboring Randolph County, where she had lived so briefly, no one had opened unquestioning arms to her as this woman had. Martitia swallowed a lump in her throat.

She went inside. So tired was she that the whole of the evening meal passed like a dream. She saw dimly the wide hearth in the long kitchen, with its hanging crane. The kitchen ran lengthwise along the house, from end to end. It opened out on both front and back. Eunice and Ruth came and went before the fire. The boys trooped in, teasing their mother about having no dog meat for supper. Martitia could not understand their nonsense. Outside sounded the barking of dogs. Voices clattered around the red-checked cloth on the dark table. Martitia ate without knowing what she ate. Eunice seemed always to see that her plate was full. The girl wondered, dimly, who the old man was at Dr. David's right hand. But no one remembered to tell her.

Then she was free at last to go upstairs, up the narrow steep steps, to a room under the roof. Ruth led the way with a candle. Of all the Gardners, Ruth seemed the most silent. She spoke only seven words to Martitia.

"I hope you will sleep well, Martitia."

Then Martitia was alone. The memories of the last six days closed over her head. She sat down on her little tin chest that Dr. David himself had brought upstairs before supper. She bowed her head, and her short, dark hair fell over on her knees. The tears would not come. Only the faces of her father and her mother burned before her shut eyes.

My father and my mother are dead. I am all alone. What is to become of me now?

For a long time she huddled so. Through the closed door she could hear voices from below, gay voices. Somewhere a clock ticked, endlessly, relentlessly. Then a quick, light knock sounded at the door. Martitia lifted dry blue eyes from her knees.

"Come in."

Eunice Gardner stood in the door. She swept the candlelit room with a searching glance. Then she came with her curiously light tread across to the tin chest and the crouching small figure there.

"My husband has told me about thy grief, Martitia. To have thy father and thy mother both leave thee in one day is a heavy affliction. But typhoid fever is not a thing which may bend always to the will of man. It is the will of God whether a man may live or die. Man must bend without question and without rebellion to that will. Come, kneel by thy bed in silence with me and suffer the spirit of God to enter our hearts."

Eunice did not touch the girl. Together they knelt on the floor. After a while Eunice went away without a word. Martitia rose and walked over to the dormer window. Summer stars stared down at her from the sky.

Words that her mother had often spoken came back to her now: "Though He slay me, yet will I trust Him."

She undressed, tumbling her tight-waisted dress and full white petticoats on the floor. She pulled back the plain homespun spread, blew out the candle, and climbed into the low spool bed. Toward the window full of stars she turned her face. She tucked both hands under her cheek.

Through the window floated the eery call of a screech owl. Tears fell on the clasped hands.

I am all alone now. What will become of me?

CHAPTER II

The House at Centre

NEXT MORNING Martitia woke late. She knew it was late by the stillness of the house and by the slant of the sun through the window. She rose hurriedly and put on her clothes. Down the steep steps she hastened. The copper toes of her small, thick shoes made a clattering sound on the bare oak boards. Down in the kitchen she found no one but the old man who had sat at Dr. David's right hand last night. He rocked by an open window.

"Please, will you tell me where I can wash my face and hands, sir?"

The old man pointed silently through the door onto the porch at the back of the house. He said nothing.

Martitia ran out on the back porch. In the shadow of the morning-glory vine she saw a shelf with a bucket of water and a tin basin on it. Above this hung a large gourd dipper and a clean towel. She took the dipper and filled the basin with water. She scrubbed her slim cheeks till they shone. Then she poured the water over the edge of the porch, dried her face and hands, and went back into the kitchen.

The old man pointed toward the fireplace. "Thy porridge is there. My daughter-in-law Eunice has gone to the springhouse with my granddaughter Ruth. They left porridge in the pot for thee. There's milk in the pitcher on the table. The bread and the butter are there too."

He stopped talking. Martitia ate her breakfast. When she had finished she pulled a zinnia from the jugful on the table. She stroked the red petals.

The old man spoke again. "Thee likes the things of this world. I know it by thy fondling of that flower. Thy face is grave and thine eyes are those of a good child. Thee loves bright colors, though, like my son David and his children. Thee is not like my daughter-in-law Eunice and me. My daughter-in-law Eunice and myself know the vanity of this world. We keep to the plain language and the plain dress and the plain ways. My son David and his children serve Mammon."

Martitia hesitated. "Are you a Quaker, sir?"

"I like not that word 'Quaker.' I am a Friend. So is my daughter-in-law Eunice. My son David was born a Friend. But he and his children have departed from the ways of plain folk. They serve Mammon. All but Miriam and Evelina and Louisa. They are the eldest. They have married and gone to Indiana to escape this curse of black slavery. This generation of young people left behind will come to no good end. They dress in bright colors; they speak like the inhabitants of this world; they laugh too much. They serve Mammon. Does thee serve Mammon, child?"

"I am a Presbyterian, sir."

The old man sat a while silently. Then he stirred. "How old is thee?"

"I am sixteen, sir."

"Don't thee 'sir' me. Call me 'Grandfather Daniel' like these godless children of my son David's."

"Yes, Grandfather Daniel."

The old man paused. Then he announced proudly: "Thee is only sixteen. But *I* am *ninety-two!*"

Martitia smiled gravely. The silence in the long kitchen was broken for a while by the humming of bees outside the window. Somewhere a lamb bleated in the hot stillness.

Martitia spoke at last. "Could I have quill and ink, Grandfather Daniel? There is a letter I must write. Upstairs in my chest I have two pieces of paper tissue. But I have no ink or quill."

"Only Jonathan uses quill and ink in this house. And only Jonathan reads books. Jonathan is gone with my son David and the other boys to lay by corn in the upland today. He will be home at midday. Thee can ask him for quill and ink then. But why does thee wish to set quill to paper for a letter, child?"

Martitia's face whitened. Her answer came very low: "I must write to my aunt in Richmond and tell her the news of my father's and mother's death."

"Is thy aunt in Richmond all the relations thee has now?"

"Yes, Grandfather Daniel."

"Will thy aunt take thee to live with her now in Richmond since thy father and thy mother are dead?" Grandfather Daniel's voice held the kind but far-away detachment of the very old.

Martitia's lips quivered. "I do not know. My aunt does not love me very dearly. My uncle-in-law is rich but he is not my own kin."

Grandfather Daniel probed on with his distant but curious old voice: "If thy aunt will not take thee to live with her in Richmond, what will thee do then? Where will thee live?"

Martitia put her head over on the table, resting her soft dark hair on the checked cloth. Her fingers curled and uncurled. The red zinnia was mashed into bright fragments and fell to the oak floor. She spoke in a thin voice.

"If my aunt will not have me, I have nowhere else to go. I do not know what will become of me."

"Thee is so young. When thee is as old as I am, thee will not worry over what the future holds. The future is all past."

Martitia raised her head from the table. "At midday I will borrow the quill and ink from Jonathan. I will write the letter. Now I wish to go to the springhouse and talk with Aunt Eunice and Ruth. Where is the springhouse, Grandfather Daniel?"

The old man pointed through the window. The girl followed with her eyes the direction he indicated. It was down the hill at the front of the house. She went out on the front porch. Down the stone steps she descended to the grassy yard. By the sun above she guessed it must be all of nine o'clock.

She walked past the Dutch oven at the left of the porch and followed a well-shaded path that led under the oak trees and pines straight down the hill at the front. Above her she heard blackbirds and meadow larks. Two blackheart cherry trees stretched wide, symmetrical branches across the path. The ground grew damper under her feet. She came to a big poplar at the foot of the slope. Under it stood what she knew must be the springhouse. It was a low pine building with a peaked roof. From inside came the sound of voices and the steady beat of a wooden dasher in a churn. She went in the door.

It was dim inside after the sunshine. Martitia blinked. A voice spoke from the cool, shadowy interior:

"So you have decided to rise up from your bed at last?" It was Ruth's clipped tones.

Another voice, warmer, quicker, interrupted: "Shame on thee, Ruth. Martitia was weary from her travels. Thee would sleep late also if thee had come all the way from Randolph County yesterday. Welcome, Martitia. Come, give me a hand with the butter. It is beginning to gather."

Martitia advanced further into the springhouse. Her eyes began to accustom themselves to the dimness. She saw a raised wooden platform beside the spring. On the platform sat Eunice with a big churn. Ruth was busy at the spring with crocks.

"I don't know how to churn or make butter, Aunt Eunice. I can't give a hand. My mother always made the butter at home."

Ruth stopped working with the crocks. "Every tub ought to stand on its own bottom."

Eunice spoke sternly: "Silence, Ruth. Thee rose from the wrong side of thy bed this morning. The butter is about made now. Show Martitia the room above, where the loom is. Mayhap the child would like to see the cloth on the loom. 'Tis a pretty pattern, set to thy father's wishes, not mine."

Ruth left the spring and pointed to a ladder at the back of the springhouse. "I'll climb the ladder first. Follow me."

Martitia climbed the ladder at Ruth's heels. Upstairs there was more light. A peaked window at the front looked out on the poplar tree. A long hand loom spread over most of the tiny room. Under the window was an earthen brazier. Some warping boards inclined against one wall. Red peppers hung in strings from the rafters. Foursquare and true stood the loom. Its roller at the front held a length of dark woolen cloth patterned in small squares.

Ruth went over and pointed to the woolen cloth.

Martitia examined the pattern. "It's beautiful. Who wove it? Was it you or Aunt Eunice?"

"Neither. Ma only finished the last yard. She will take it from the loom soon. But 'twas Louisa who wove it. She was the family weaver."

"I know that Louisa is your older sister. Grandfather Daniel told me that Louisa had gone to Indiana to live. When did she go? Since her cloth is still in the loom, she must have been here till recently."

"Louisa married last month. Her husband William took her to Indiana. They went with a caravan of Friends who were leaving Jamestown near by us. Haply their wagon has already reached Wayne County where my sister Miriam and my sister Evelina are already settled with their families.

"Who will do the weaving now that Louisa has gone?"

"I don't rightly know. I know how to weave plain weaves well enough. But all wintertime I am in school. Ma could do it, but she's uncommon busy with the cook-

ing and butter-making and the poultry. I don't know who
will do our weaving now."

"My mother sometimes wove beautiful cloth. Though
mostly she contrived to get lengths of other folks' weaving."

"Can *you* weave?"

"No. My mother wished me to keep my hands soft for
the spinet and for painting pictures."

"Every tub ought to stand on its own bottom." Ruth
flounced back to the ladder head and disappeared down
the square opening. Martitia followed her.

Downstairs Eunice was washing the butter. Ruth
helped dexterously. Martitia watched them.

"In winter," said Eunice, "I make the butter at the
house. In summer 'tis easier to work close to the spring
with the milk and butter."

Presently the three women climbed the slope to the
house.

Grandfather Daniel had fallen asleep in his chair. On
the table Martitia's breakfast dishes still stood unwashed.
Ruth looked at them. She looked at Martitia. Martitia
flushed. Ruth walked over and examined the crumpled
brown flower petals lying on the immaculate floor. Eunice
was already busy about the fireplace.

Ruth mumbled, too low for her mother to hear but
not too low for Martitia to understand: "Small hands are
too white, I reckon, for washing dishes or for picking up
trash. Every tub ought to stand on its own bottom."

Martitia turned and fled up the stairs. She went to the
spool bed and awkwardly made it up. She straightened
the room in a desultory fashion. She emptied her tin
trunk and tumbled things into the chest of drawers.

When she came to two sheets of thin letter paper she placed them on top of the chest. Then she smoothed her hair. There was no mirror to tell her how she looked. She sat down by the window and stared disconsolately at the sky.

It was not that Ruth was really unkind, she decided. How could an independent girl like Ruth understand a girl who had never learned to wash or sweep or churn or weave?

Martitia stared down at the slim, small hands in her lap. She recollected sadly how often her mother had said: "I want your hands to stay small and white and soft, Martitia. My own were like that once. Look at them now."

Martitia's eyes blurred. She wished Dr. David and the boys would come back from the upland. She wished Jonathan would come home and lend her his quill and ink to write to her aunt in Richmond with. To be alone was dreadful. Suppose her aunt wouldn't let her come to live with her in Richmond! Suppose she were always to be alone like this! Suppose she lived to be as old as Grandfather Daniel!

It was noon before the boys and Dr. David came trooping back. Martitia heard them and ran downstairs. With them laughter returned to the house in great waves. They stood on the back porch and washed mightily at the basin. Their blue-jean trousers and homespun shirts were wet with July sweat. They stomped into Eunice's clean kitchen with their black and brown heads slicked and shining. Martitia watched them and felt warmth flow back into her veins.

Dr. David patted her head. "You look better than last

night, child. Come eat a good dinner with me." He made Martitia sit at his left side.

The boys ate enormously, gazing sometimes sidewise at Martitia. She mostly kept her eyes on her plate.

Clarkson alone addressed the newcomer directly. "Look at Addison's ears, Martitia. See how they've grown since you saw them at supper last night? Addison has been eating dog meat all morning instead of laying by corn. Addison is getting to have dog ears."

The boys and Dr. David roared. Eunice smiled. Only Ruth and Grandfather Daniel kept grave. Martitia wished she could understand this nonsense about dog meat.

After dinner was over she screwed her courage to the sticking point. She approached Jonathan. "Please, Jonathan, would you lend me your quill and ink to write a letter with?"

Jonathan stared down at her. His hazel eyes twinkled. "Do you know how to spell, Martitia? Could you write a whole letter without spelling a great many words wrong?"

Martitia reddened. "How did you know I couldn't spell very well?"

Jonathan grinned. "I know a great many things about you that you might wonder at. Wait till tonight to write your letter. I'll help you then when I'm through with my work. You can have my quill and ink to use. I'll correct your spelling. Studying Latin to be a lawyer has sharpened my powers at spelling."

Martitia stared at the powerful, smiling mouth. She measured the indomitable purpose in those hazel eyes. "All right, Jonathan. You can help with the spelling."

Jonathan brought out his quill and ink after supper that evening. He put another candle on the table in the kitchen when Ruth and Eunice had cleared up and washed. The others went out on the porch. He and Martitia sat down in two high-backed wooden chairs.

"I will write the whole letter, Jonathan. Then when I am finished, you can correct it."

"As you like."

Jonathan stayed very still in the candlelight. When Martitia looked up sometimes from her paper tissue and quill she found his keen eyes studying her.

She finished the letter at last. Jonathan took it gravely and read it.

> *At the Gardner House*
> *Near Centre, North Carolina*
> *20th July, 1831*

MISSTRESS MARGARET RANDOLPH
RICHMOND, VIRGINIA

DEAR AUNT MARGARET,

My mother died last Tuesday of typhoid fevre. My father lived only four hours after her. They had not been ill very long. Dr. David Gardner of Centre was called over to Asheborough to attend them. He was too late to do anything. He brought me home with him after the funerul. My mother and father were buried in the Presbiterian burying ground in Asheborough. I am all alone now.

Doctor David Gardner is a good man, a Quaker. He says I am to stay here with his family till I hear from you. There was nobody in Asheborough who cared about keeping me, since we were strangers there. I know you did not appruve of my father's selling out in Richmond and coming to the wilds of North Carolina. But maybe since he is dead, you will forgiv him and take me to live with you in Rich-

mond. My mother said you would be willing to have me for her sake.

My father left forty dollars in hand. He had bought a small house in Asheborough with the rest of what he had. My father couldn't find much busyness during the two months we were in Asheborough. A clock-salesman did not seem to be needed there.

Will you write to me in care of Dr. David Gardner at Centre to say whether I may come to live with you? And will you tell me when to expect Uncle James to come and fetch me?

Your respectful neice,
MARTITIA HOWLAND

Jonathan corrected the childish handwriting with a neat copperplate script. He returned the result. There was no laughter in his eyes.

"My father will see that your letter is carried over to the Jamestown coach. You need have no fear. It may be six weeks, though, before you get a reply from Virginia. The posts are slow down here in Carolina."

Martitia sighed deeply.

Jonathan hesitated; then he spoke swiftly: "If thy aunt does not bid thee come to Richmond, Martitia, thee must not feel alone. My father and my mother will keep thee."

Martitia felt the tears slipping down her cheeks in the candlelight. Jonathan's words had caught her unawares with their sudden lapse into the Quaker speech of his mother. His "thee" and "thy" undid her thin defenses. She could not answer him. She only stared at him dumbly in the candlelight, with the tears tangled in her long lashes.

CHAPTER III

Festival of the Dog

MARTITIA SAT on the front steps of Dr. David's house in the early afternoon sunlight. Above her a blackbird was singing. It was the third week of her stay at Centre. She wore a plain white muslin dress.

"Thee is too young to dye thy clothes black, Martitia. Thy mother would not wish it." Eunice had settled thus the question of Martitia's clothes.

Martitia sat alone now and listened to the blackbird singing. For almost the first time since she had said goodby to her mother and father she felt her mouth curve into a faint smile. The smile held no humor, only a grave sweetness. Here on the steps the sun was warm. Bees hummed in the zinnia beds. The blackbird sang on and on.

Then the dreamy quiet of the yard was pierced by a salvo of loud voices, the clatter of horses' hoofs, and the barking of dogs. Martitia shrank back against the stone

31

steps. Those boys were home again from one of their frequent rides to heaven-knew-where!

They came galloping up to the steps, all five of them, on horseback. Dogs leaped at the horses' heels. Three of the boys got down in a great jumble of big shoes and blue jeans and touseled shocks of hair. Addison and Barzillai stayed in their saddles and led the other riderless horses off toward the barn. The five dogs barked joyously after them.

Milton, Clarkson, and Jonathan approached Martitia on the steps. Clarkson smiled.

"It's very fitting that you are dressed in white, Martitia. You are going to attend the Festival of the Dog with us."

Martitia paled. She looked at Jonathan and Milton. Their faces were bland and solemn.

"Must I go whether I want to go or not?"

"Yes." Clarkson's voice was firm.

"Where is the Festival to take place, and who will be there?"

"Over yonder, down beyond Polecat Creek." Clarkson pointed a thumb vaguely down the hill. "It's just us who will be there."

"Does Aunt Eunice know about the Festival? Did she say that I must go?"

Milton answered energetically: "Ma sometimes goes to the Festival of the Dog herself. Pa does too. If they hadn't walked over to the Macys' house with Ruth, I reckon Pa and Ma would both have gone. But somehow"—Milton stammered slightly—"somehow we boys forgot to remind them it was the day for the Festival. Now it's your bounden duty, Martitia, to go to the Festival alone and represent the Gardner womenfolk."

Martitia studied each face. They looked back at her solemnly.

Jonathan spoke quietly. "Go tell Grandfather Daniel you are going with us to the Festival, Martitia. We'll wait for you here."

"Yes, Jonathan." Martitia turned and went obediently inside to the kitchen.

Grandfather Daniel roused from his nap by the window. "Going to the Festival of the Dog, eh? If I were five years younger I'd go too. Many's the year I've helped with the Festival of the Dog on Nantucket." His eyes smoldered with momentary interest. He yawned. His lids closed.

Martitia hurried out into the yard. Addison and Barzillai had come up from the barn now and had joined Milton and Clarkson and Jonathan. The five boys stood in a circle with their heads close together. They drew apart hastily when they saw Martitia coming. Their five faces looked at her with extremest gravity. Addison held a basket over one arm.

"Are you ready?" Barzillai's slow voice sounded almost funereal.

Addison's large ears twitched. Milton and Clarkson cleared their throats. Jonathan said nothing.

Down the path to the springhouse the five boys went. They made Martitia go ahead of them.

"How long will the Festival of the Dog last?" Martitia flung back timidly.

"Children should be seen and not heard," answered Addison.

Martitia flushed. "I'm not a child, Addison. I'm a year older than you are."

Clarkson began to chant aloud in a clear tenor voice:

> *"Of all the Gardners under the sun*
> *Jonathan Gardner is twenty-one.*
> *Milton has lived enough and plenty,*
> *Milton Gardner will soon be twenty.*
> *Clarkson's hair is raven black;*
> *Eighteen years he's combed it back.*
> *Barzillai's eyes are long and green,*
> *Barzillai's all of seventeen.*
> *And every bit of fifteen years*
> *Addison's worn those great big ears."*

The boys took up the chant one by one. They seemed to Martitia to be familiar with the words already. The chant rose and fell as they walked. Bushes and brambles tore at Martitia's white muslin dress. She wiped perspiration in streams from her flushed face.

"We're coming to Polecat Creek now." Clarkson looked at Martitia. The woods were dense about the path.

"Are there polecats here?" inquired the girl worriedly.

"Polecats and wildcats and sometimes wolves." Barzillai sounded as though wolves were nothing to be excited about in Guilford County.

"Must we cross Polecat Creek?"

"Of course, Martitia. You aren't afraid of lizards and water moccasins and leeches, are you?" Addison wiggled one ear unconcernedly.

Martitia stopped abruptly in the path. "I think I feel sort of faint with the heat. I'd better go back home without going to the Festival."

Clarkson took her elbow lightly but firmly. "Come on, Martitia. It's not much further now. The Festival is going to be held just beyond Polecat Creek. You'll get something good to eat then from Addison's basket. He's got the lunch."

They approached the muddy waters of a creek. There was no footbridge over the water. Some big stones stood up from the creek bed near the shore. Further out the stones joined a huge fallen log lying across the rest of the stream.

Jonathan and Milton and Barzillai negotiated the stones and the slippery log with practiced skill. They called back gayly:

"Come on, Martitia. Your turn is next."

Clarkson bowed to Martitia. "Ladies first." He pointed to the stones and the log.

Addison bowed also. "Women and children first." He stood aside.

Martitia accepted the inevitable. She set a timid shoe on the first stone in the water.

Clarkson inquired interestedly of Addison: "I wonder if the big moccasin still lives under these stones?"

Martitia drew back violently. Clarkson gave her a helpful lift. Martitia was forced to go on out over the stones. Step by step she teetered toward the slippery log. As she reached the edge of the log Milton suddenly cried out from the other side of the creek: "Watch out, Martitia, there's a lizard coming up the log toward your foot!"

Martitia teetered wildly. She tried to turn and go back toward the bank of the creek from which she had come. Like a windmill she waved her seesawing arms. She could not negotiate the turn though. She was forced to push forward. The wet log under her shoes slipped and slithered.

Milton cried out again agonizedly: "Be careful, Martitia! If you fall into that deep water you'll be covered with leeches. They'll hang to your skin and suck out your blood."

Martitia clenched the hands on both seesawing arms. Her face drained white of blood. She floundered and flapped weakly across the remaining length of endless-seeming log. She achieved the solid earth. She sank to the ground without a word. Her spattered white skirts spread out around her like the petals of a bedraggled flower.

Clarkson and Addison raced and leaped across the creek behind her. Ahead Jonathan and Milton and Barzillai started walking again. "Come on, Martitia." Their five voices seemed to mingle into an irresistible unison.

Martitia rose and followed them.

They came presently to an open clearing under the sky. A pile of large stones formed a sort of fireplace in the center. It had rather the look, Martitia thought, of a sacrificial funeral pyre. She had a moment's wild impulse to flee. Maybe these unaccountable and fearful boys meant to sacrifice her on these stones. She controlled her imagination with an effort.

Addison put his basket down in the clearing. Hot as the afternoon was, Milton, Jonathan, Barzillai, Clarkson, and Addison set themselves to gathering twigs and branches for the obvious purpose of building a fire among the stones. Soon, with the aid of flint and steel, the five boys had a fire burning. Addison uncovered the basket and hung some chunks of meat on a rough spit over the flames. The five boys sat down and watched the meat cooking.

Jonathan approached Martitia after a while where she huddled on the ground near by. The other boys gathered around in a circle. Jonathan seemed to be the master of ceremonies.

"We have permitted you, Martitia, to be an honored guest at a family institution. This is the day set aside each year in the Gardner family for the celebration of the Festival of the Dog. It is a solemn and eventful time." He paused.

The other four boys nodded their heads portentously.

Jonathan continued: "The dog is a noble animal. The dog deserves to be commemorated yearly by the Gardner family for an act of surpassing value in the history of our Gardner ancestors. The story is a tale of danger, of hardships, and of triumphant courage."

"Hear, hear!" intoned the four other boys like a Greek chorus.

"The Festival of the Dog has been continued in an unbroken line for nearly two hundred years in our Gardner family. All but you, Martitia, know the story of its origin. For your sake I will tell the tale again. Our Nantucket ancestors were whalers. A whaling voyage once carried them to the Arctic, where they added a pack of Arctic dogs, of huskies, to their cargo of whale oil. On the return trip home they were delayed by adverse winds and storms. Provisions of food gave out. They were faced with the problem of eat dog or starve. They decided to eat dog! And at the end of the voyage only one dog remained intact. The lives of our ancestors were saved, and the Festival of the Dog was instituted in commemoration of the service rendered by the dogs on that eventful voyage. For two hundred years since the Gardner descendants have eaten dog each year to commemorate that event."

Jonathan paused dramatically. He turned and sniffed the air like one of the great huskies he had just described. "Addison, you are custodian of this year's feast. Is this year's dog meat done to a turn on the spit yonder?"

Addison retired to the fire. He shifted the meat on the spit and sniffed importantly. He returned to the others. "Dog meat is ready. Advance to the Feast."

The five boys marched over to the fire. Martitia sat still on the ground and watched them. Each boy gravely took a piece of meat from the spit as Addison tore it. They began to eat. Martitia's pale face turned paler still. She twisted her mouth and swallowed hard. She watched them in a dreadful fascination. When the five boys had done eating they came over to Martitia.

Jonathan spoke: "Come get your share of dog meat, Martitia. Come eat dog with us."

Martitia shivered. She turned her face away. She sat perfectly still on the ground.

Jonathan left the rest and went over to the fire. He came back carrying a slice of meat. He knelt by Martitia and said: "Open your mouth, Martitia. Eat dog."

Martitia rose up suddenly from the ground, knocking the meat from Jonathan's hand. Her face turned green. Her chin contorted. Her chest heaved. She clapped both small hands over her anguished mouth and fled for the bushes at the side of the clearing.

From behind the hazel bushes she could hear the boys laughing. She was too sick to care. She leaned her head against a tree trunk. She stayed there a long time.

When she came back slowly into the clearing the

boys were sitting in a ring around the extinguished fire, talking. Martitia stared at them. They rose and came in a bunch to her.

"If you feel all right now, Martitia, we'll be going home. It's getting late." Clarkson looked slightly red.

Martitia turned without a word and started off up the path alone. The five boys followed her. For a while they were strangely silent. Soon their laughter returned, however. By the time they neared Polecat Creek they were as boisterous as ever.

Martitia waited for them to catch up with her at the edge of the creek. She stood, small and wan and bedraggled, before the slippery log. Jonathan came up first. He looked down at Martitia with irrepressible amusement lurking in his hazel eyes.

"So little you are, Martitia. So little and so solemn. If you would only laugh back at us maybe we'd let you alone. Can't you learn to laugh too?"

Martitia refused to answer him.

He leaned over and picked her up lightly. "Come, Martitia, I'll carry you across the stream."

He walked out surely on the log, with Martitia held in his easy grasp. She felt secure at last. No lurking leeches and lizards and moccasin snakes could get her now. She relaxed with a sigh in his arms.

Then, right in the middle of the stream, Jonathan jumped over into the creek with her!

It was as sudden as that. One minute she was held securely dry and safe in Jonathan's arms on the log. Next minute she was scrambling and pawing in the waters of the creek. Martitia felt the warm, muddy stream engulf her short body to the waist. She wondered, wildly, if moccasins and leeches and lizards were feeding on her already. She splashed her hands up and down till water spattered in sheets up into her drenched face. Blind with water, she struggled toward the bank of the creek. Slipping and weeping she reached the edge. She stood there a minute, her muslin dress dankly dripping. Then without a backward look at her tormentors she fled weeping up the path in the direction of home.

Behind her the sound of giant laughter pursued her all the way to the springhouse.

CHAPTER IV

Martitia Sets a Goal

FOR THE NEXT WEEK Martitia avoided the Gardner boys. They went their way, laughing and noisy. She
stayed close to Eunice in the kitchen and in the cool
springhouse down the hill. Often she listened to Grandfather Daniel's stories of his early days on Nantucket Island.
She rode twice to the settlement at Centre, a mile and a
half away, with Dr. David in his gig. Once it was to attend
Meeting on First Day with Eunice and Dr. David. Once it
was to visit Christian Swain's tanyard to get a new saddle
for Eunice's white horse. She walked over one day with
Eunice to the Macys' house near by. With Eunice she felt
gravely secure. With Dr. David she basked in a warm
glow. No word had come yet from her aunt in Richmond.
She longed, yet she feared, for the sight of that letter.
What irretrievable news would it contain?

Martitia tried to steer clear of Ruth as much as possible. One morning in mid-August, though, Martitia ran
aground of Ruth. She had gone up to clean her room

under the eaves. Armed with a bundle of broomstraw, she swept the bare oak boards. The door into the hall was ajar. Martitia approached the chest of drawers by the window. There was no mirror over the chest, but there was a rag rug of dark color underneath. She reached the rug. She lifted the rug and swept the accumulation of dust underneath. Then she returned the rug to its accustomed place and straightened up.

A clipped voice addressed her from the open door: "So that's the way little girls with white hands sweep up a floor? Little girls with white hands can't be bothered with carrying the trash downstairs in a pan. Little girls with white hands just sweep the dust under a rug and hide it there."

Martitia grew scarlet. She faced Ruth in the doorway. "I didn't know anyone was watching me."

"Haven't you got enough pride in your own soul to want to do a job right whether anyone's watching you or not?"

Martitia's head drooped. The short, dark hair shadowed her cheeks. She stood silent.

Ruth bustled into the room. She sat down on Martitia's tin trunk. "I'd be ashamed to be as helpless as you are, Martitia. A grown girl of sixteen who can't even sweep a floor or churn butter or weave a strip of wool cloth. I'll reckon you can't even make a loaf of bread, can you?"

"No." Martitia's answer muffled itself in her hair.

"I thought you couldn't. I could make bread when I was ten. I learned to weave when I was twelve. Now that I'm fourteen I can keep house as well as Ma nearly. Can you even *sew*, Martitia?"

"No." Martitia mumbled the word.

"Is there *anything* you can do besides fold your hands in your lap?"

"I can play the spinet. I can paint pictures. My mother taught me both those things. I can also speak the language the French people speak."

Ruth snorted. "You're not like to find spinets to play in good folks' houses. There's none here at Pa's. As for painting pictures, that's sinful. What use is it to speak the language the French people speak unless you live where the French people do?"

Martitia could think of no answer to this. She remained silent. Her checks looked as though they would burn themselves away.

Ruth surveyed her, a puzzled expression on her sturdy, pronounced features. "Why were you brought up to be so useless and ignorant, Martitia?"

Martitia turned toward the window. She answered with her back toward the girl on the trunk. The slow, sensitive voice hesitated often. "My mother had a wish for me to be raised as she was raised. She didn't want me to work hard like she did. When my mother was a young girl she lived in a handsome house near Richmond and had slaves to wait on her. She played the spinet and painted fine miniatures. But then she married my father because she loved him. And my father was not a very good hand at making money." Martitia paused a long time here before she would go on. "Sometimes we had a servant; sometimes we had none. So my mother learned to clean and to cook. Her slim little hands grew stiff and big-knuckled. She wished dreadfully for my hands not to become like hers. It was a symbol, she said. I didn't choose to sit idle. 'Twas just that my mother wished it so." The voice broke off with a quick, indrawn breath.

The girl on the trunk was silent a minute. She broke out at last: "Every tub ought to stand on its own bottom. But I'm sorry I spoke to you so, Martitia. 'Tisn't your fault that you can't do anything. *You're* not the one to blame."

Martitia turned from the window swiftly and looked straight into Ruth's eyes. "If you're thinking that it's my mother's fault, you're welcome to leave this room this very minute!"

It was Ruth who flushed now. Her voice came quick and full of compunction: "I ask thy pardon, Martitia. I meant not to speak ill or to think ill of thy mother. Thee must forgive my sharp tongue."

Martitia knew bewilderment at the soft Quaker language of Ruth. These unaccountable people in the hip-roofed house! How oddly they fell into the tender "thee" and "thy" of their mother when they were deeply moved! It was so that Jonathan had spoken to her in the candle-light her second night at Centre.

She put out her hand. "You are forgiven. Please, though, won't you go away and leave me alone now? I want to think out some thoughts in my own head."

Ruth left without a word. Her swift, determined footsteps died away down the stairs.

Martitia went over to the chest of drawers. She took out something from under a tumbled pile of garments in the bottom drawer. She went over to the chair by the window and sat down. She stared at the object in her fingers. A gold-rimmed brooch shone in the light from the window. Martitia studied the brooch. A small miniature was painted delicately on its ivory oval. From within the gold rim a face looked back at Martitia. The face in the miniature was the face of a child of apparently eleven or twelve. Grave blue eyes, thickly lashed, looked out from a slim, pointed face. The delicate dark eyebrows above were curved like swallows' wings. Dark straight hair, parted in the middle, was drawn back from the small ears by a blue ribbon. The hair came only halfway to the shoulders. Soft lips turned slightly down at the corners. The chin beneath was strangely firm for so sensitive a mouth.

But what gave the painted face its odd charm was the upper eyelids. They were slightly heavy and drooped a little over the eyes, as though they were too tired to open entirely.

Martitia stared at the miniature.

Was I like that when my mother painted me so? Am I like that now? Where is my mother? Will I truly ever see her again?

She sat a long time, staring at the miniature. If this was all that was left of the talent and charm and grace of her mother, was it not right to stare at it now? Was it not wise to memorize the picture that her mother had painted and worn to the day of her death on her always shabby but always lovely dress? If her mother had so cherished and valued this little painted picture of her daughter, was it not right for that daughter to value it too? Martitia stared at her own painted self in the miniature. She could scarcely see the gold-rimmed face for her tears. After a while she put the brooch back in the drawer. She sat down at the window again and stared out unseeingly.

You are gone now. You will never paint miniatures of your little daughter again with your gentle, big-knuckled fingers. You will never bake and sweep and wash again for your little useless loving daughter. What will that daughter do now?

The girl in the chair lifted her hands suddenly from her blue homespun lap. She examined those hands curiously, as though she had never seen them before. If they could play a spinet and hold a paintbrush, what other mysterious and useful things could those hands do?

Martitia rose in a rush of blue homespun and white petticoats. She bent over her tin trunk. She took out a portfolio of water-color drawings. She examined them intently for a long time. In a small voice she announced at last to the trunk: "I never truly had talent like my mother. I only copied dimly what my mother drew well." She determinedly put back the packet of pictures in the very bottom of the trunk with a gesture of dismissal.

Then she went to the chest of drawers, got her hairbrush, and brushed her dark hair neatly. She retied the narrow blue ribbon about her head. She smoothed out her tight bodice, straightened the gathers in the full skirt that just cleared her small ankles, and pulled her black stockings up neatly.

Then she went to the door, opened it quietly, and walked in a slow and orderly fashion down the stairs. In the kitchen she looked about for Eunice. But Eunice had gone out to the yard to the Dutch oven used in the summer. Martitia could see her through the window. So Martitia went out to the oven too. She passed the well in her progress. She paused long enough to drink a draught of well water from the swinging bucket. Then she approached Eunice. Eunice was kneeling before the half-cylinder of bricks that formed the Dutch oven. She was drawing out a heavy brick pan full of beaten biscuits.

Martitia addressed her firmly: "Aunt Eunice, I want to learn how to cook. Will you teach me how? I want to learn to be useful like you and Ruth."

Eunice rose, balancing the heavy pan adroitly. "Come inside with me, child. It's nigh twelve o'clock by the sun. I must blow the cow's horn to tell David and the boys to come in from stacking the hay. Hungry menfolk wait for naught of women's talk. When dinner is done and the kitchen redded up I'll consider thy problem then."

Eunice's dinner of savory mutton and squash and cabbage and biscuits was shoveled into nine ravenous mouths. Martitia watched Dr. David and the five boys eating enormously. She ate too. Eunice went out once more to the oven and brought back a platter of hot apple pies shaped like little half-moons. The boys and Dr. David descended upon the pies jubilantly.

"This is better than dog meat, isn't it, Martitia?" inquired Jonathan between mouthfuls of apple and sugary pastry. He flicked one eyelid over its hazel eye.

The other four boys snickered. Martitia refused to answer or to smile. The boys and Dr. David went trooping out to the back yard and lay under the trees for a while. Martitia heard their sleepy talk through the window. Presently she saw them leave for the fields again, for what still remained to Martitia the infinite mysteries of haystacking or fodder-pulling or corn-hoeing or sheep-tending.

Ruth silently helped her mother redd up the kitchen. Martitia watched the two women wash and dry and put things to rights. For the first time in four weeks her eyes followed their every motion. If one was to learn the intricacies of housekeeping one must watch and study. Ruth went away finally in the direction of the springhouse.

Eunice got out a basket that overflowed with thick socks. She sat down at the table, her needle poised. "Come, child. Let us consider thy problem of learning the ways of a cook oven and a stew pot. Why has thee come to so sturdy a determination in thy small head?"

Martitia spoke quickly: "Aunt Eunice, I am tired of knowing nothing to do with my useless hands but finger a spinet's keys or handle a paintbrush. I want to be like you and Ruth. Your hands and Ruth's hands know how to do sensible things, useful things. My hands know nothing." She held them up for Eunice to look at.

Eunice lowered the sock she was mending. She surveyed the hands. "Pretty little hands they are. Handsome is as handsome does, though. Hands must earn their right to live."

"Until I go to Richmond to live with my aunt Margaret Randolph I don't wish to be beholden to you for all I eat and drink. I want to stand on my own bottom."

Eunice nodded her cap in agreement.

Martitia went on: "I want to learn to cook and sew and clean. Will you teach me?"

Eunice looked shrewdly across her darning gourd. "Isn't thee a little bit lazy, though, Martitia?"

Martitia flushed. "Yes, Aunt Eunice. I am somewhat lazy."

"Honest confession is good for the soul, child. Thee can approach thy problem squarely now. If I am to teach thee to cook and sew and clean thee will have to work hard."

"I will work hard, Aunt Eunice. Try me and see."

"Very well, then, Martitia. While thee remains with us at Centre I will take thee in hand and teach thee housewifery."

Martitia sprang up. "Let me start this minute. Let me learn to make half-moon apple pies."

"Tut, tut, child. Thee will have to start with loaf bread and collards and turnips. Half-moon apple pies come a deal of a time later on."

CHAPTER V

Flour and Salt

NEXT MORNING, after her conversation with Eunice, Martitia jumped up at the first cockcrow. She hurried into her clothes neatly and descended the stairs. In the kitchen Eunice was already at work. Almost it seemed to the visitor that Eunice never stopped working. Eunice nodded her immaculate muslin cap at Martitia and went on with what she was doing. Martitia went out on the back porch to wash her face. There was no water yet in the big pitcher under the morning-glory vine. Martitia saw Jonathan come around the side of the house from the direction of the well. He carried two buckets of water. The buckets brimmed bright drops as they swung.

Martitia stood on the back steps and watched Jonathan come. All around her the early sweet air teemed with farm sounds. She sniffed the faint warm fragrance of morning-glories and grass and sunflowers. Morning mist still hung over the oaks and poplars. Points of dew tipped the grass blades.

Jonathan came up the steps, his splendid forehead shining in the early sunshine. He appeared overcome at sight of the girl. "Are you really up at this hour, Martitia? Or am I dreaming?" He blinked his keen hazel eyes in alarm.

Martitia frowned. She walked over to the shelf that held the pitcher and basin. She came back bearing the tin basin. "Please, Jonathan, will you fill the basin for me? I must wash my face. I'm going to help Aunt Eunice in the kitchen. I haven't time to listen to your nonsense."

"Help Aunt Eunice in the kitchen?" Jonathan looked at her with his lantern jaws very solemn. He put down the buckets. He turned his sparely built body over on his hands and stood on his head. He wiggled his feet in the air.

Martitia did not smile.

Jonathan got up and grasped one of the buckets with both hands. "Hold out your basin, Martitia. I'll fill it for you."

Martitia held out her basin. Jonathan began pouring. He poured and he poured. The clear water approached the brim of the basin. Jonathan did not stop pouring. He continued to send a bright cataract of well water into Martitia's basin. Over the brim poured the descending flood. It ran down in a sheet on Martitia's black shoes. It wetted all the floor at her feet. It spattered on her black stockings. It dampened her hem.

Martitia wailed: "Can't you *ever* let me alone? Oh, Jonathan, *please* stop pouring!"

Jonathan stopped pouring. He surveyed Martitia surprisedly. "Who would have thought that basin was so little? I never reckoned it held so small an amount of water. As a prospective lawyer I'll have to be more careful in my estimate next time." He walked off quietly. But Martitia saw his big shoulders shake under his neat home-spun shirt.

She set down the dripping basin and fled through the door to the kitchen. She went upstairs and took off her drenched shoes and stockings. Since she had no other shoes to put on she was forced to come back downstairs barefooted. Jonathan was nowhere to be seen. Ruth had joined her mother in the kitchen. Ruth looked at Marti-tia's bare toes. Martitia saw an approving glance in her direction from Ruth.

"That's very sensible of you, Martitia, to go without shoes. Foot leather is better than shoe leather, and a deal easier to repair."

Martitia set about helping in the kitchen. But the shining joy of her morning's adventure was gone, washed away by Jonathan's well water. She worked awkwardly and as silently as Ruth.

"Pa," inquired Jonathan at breakfast a while later, "isn't it extra healthful to go barefoot in summertime? Espe-cially for young females?"

Dr. David peered at his eldest son. He looked at Martitia, whose face had grown scarlet. He looked down at Martitia's bare toes where she sat in her chair at his left hand. One black eyebrow quirked. "For whatever reason a female goes barefoot, it's very healthful for her and for her menfolks' pocketbooks."

Martitia choked on her light bread. She kept her eyes determinedly on her plate. A faint wave of snickers swept around the red-checked cloth.

After breakfast, with the kitchen cleared of menfolks, Eunice set to work instructing Martitia in cooking and cleaning. Ruth showed her scant shrift. But Eunice seemed inexhaustible in her patience at guiding Martitia's unaccustomed fingers in the lore of cook pot and dishpan, lye soap and broomstraw. She insisted that Martitia do each act thoroughly and perfectly. Martitia did and undid her awkward efforts.

She was rewarded by Eunice's words after supper that evening: "Thee has been right helpful about the kitchen and springhouse all day, Martitia. Thee has only run away once. Tonight I will let thee help me set the light bread to rise till morning."

Martitia watched Eunice get the ferment out of the crockery jug and mix it deftly with the flour, the milk and water, and the salt. Eunice added a skillful dash of sugar. She kneaded the dough thoroughly in her powerful hands. Then she put it in a great crockery jug, half full, and covered it neatly. She set it near the hearth to rise.

"Tomorrow the dough will have doubled itself. Then we will knead it again to break the bubbles. We will let it rise once more till it doubles itself in the brick pans yet again. Then we will cook the loaves outside in the oven. Thee and I must recall to bake it at just the right time. For if the dough rises too long, the bread will be full of holes. If it rises too little, the bread will be heavy. And the second rising must not be done in a place where 'tis too hot, or our loaves will bear a heavy streak near the bottom. Thee and I must fashion light loaves, finely grained, and browned to a turn. Eh, Martitia?"

Martitia smiled back at the little Quaker woman. She went to bed, a contented look on her slim face. But once

on the spool bed she wiggled both battered and tired feet
with relief.

Martitia stuck at her self-imposed task of learning
housewifery. She worked hard to overcome her laziness.
Grandfather Daniel, from his chair by the kitchen window, watched interestedly all Martitia's struggles with
housekeeping. He listened to her accounts of the butter-
making down the hill. Two long, hard weeks went by.

There came the evening when Eunice turned to the
girl after supper. "Tonight, Martitia, I will suffer thee to
make the dough and raise the bread loaves all of thine
own making. Not one finger will I interfere to show thee
or to alter thy doing."

Martitia got out the ferment, the flour and salt, the
water and milk, and the sugar. She kneaded the mass of
dough carefully. Her small tongue was caught tightly in
her even teeth. She worked till a pink flush warmed her
face and dampened the dark hair at her temples. Carefully she set the crockery bowl, half full, on the hearth to
rise till morning.

In the morning she rose before all the rest of the
household and ran down to inspect her bread. Roundly
risen, bubbly and seething, was the warm mass in the
crockery bowl. At the proper time Martitia kneaded her
dough again and shaped it for second rising. She divided
the dough into four parts. Each part she kneaded till
smooth, avoiding seams underneath. These she shaped
to loaves, and put two loaves each into the two brick
pans, which she had neatly greased. Then she brushed
melted butter between each loaf. She saw to it that her
loaves but half filled their pans. Then she covered the
pans for their second rising.

When Martitia's loaves were baked in the Dutch oven Eunice watched her take the pans from the fire. Golden-brown and firm and light looked the loaves.

Eunice nodded approval. "Thy loaves look well raised, Martitia. I think thee was born to be a good housewife. Thy hands have done a useful thing this day."

Martitia went behind the Dutch oven and wept three tears. Then she hurried into the house with her bread. When the Gardners gathered at noon one of Martitia's loaves was cool enough to cut. The family ate mightily. The bread disappeared.

Grandfather Daniel broke forth at the end of the meal: "Thee should know, David, that it was the child Martitia who fashioned the loaf of bread of thy eating this day. All with her own hands she mixed and kneaded and baked the bread. 'Tis good bread, likewise; fine bread, tasty and light." Grandfather Daniel sounded proud.

At Grandfather Daniel's words everybody at the table but Martitia and Ruth and Eunice looked startled.

Dr. David patted Martitia's shoulder with quick warmth. "You are a good child, Martitia. The bread is elegant bread. 'Tis even better than your aunt Eunice's." He twinkled a naughty look at Eunice.

Eunice smiled indulgently. Martitia looked at the five boys. They remained silent. Not one of them referred to Martitia's beautiful bread loaf. The girl's sensitive lips drooped disappointedly. Her small chin quivered. Everybody rose.

"The boys and I are not going back to the fields today, Eunice. I've got to ride over and see how Nathan Coffin's broken leg is knitting. The boys can have a half day to follow out their own wickednesses." Dr. David stood by the table and wiped his mouth with the back of one large, hairy hand.

The five boys, as though by unspoken consent, retired through the door that led from the kitchen to the spare bedroom on the first floor.

In a moment Addison reappeared at the door and addressed his father. His big ears wiggled. "Pa, will you come in here a minute? It's important."

Dr. David went with Addison into the spare bedroom. Addison closed the door behind them carefully. Martitia, Ruth, and Eunice set to work clearing the table. Before the three women had got the dishpan filled and the plates scraped Dr. David came back out of the spare bedroom alone. He sat down in a straight wooden chair and watched the women work.

Eunice paused in her quick, light movements. "I thought thee said thee was going to ride over and tend to Nathan Coffin's broken leg, David. What ails thee, sitting there with thy hands folded at midday? Is thee sick?"

Dr. David only smiled. "I think I'll watch somebody else work for a spell. And I want to see that Pa doesn't go to sleep too quick after a meal. 'Tisn't good for his heart or his innards at his age."

Grandfather Daniel began to splutter at the window. "If thee has as good innards and heart as thy old father has at ninety-two, David, thee'll be luckier than I think thee'll be. Any man who serves Mammon like thee does at fifty-five is not like to live to be ninety-two. Thee uses the language of this world and thee approves bright colors about the house. Worst of all, thee laughs too much. Thee serves Mammon."

Dr. David chuckled. As he opened his great, teasing

mouth to answer, an ominous sound floated through the closed door from the spare bedroom. The sound was at first low, but it gathered volume with rapidity. It sounded as though someone were moaning. The moaning rose to a crescendo.

Dr. David jumped up and ran toward the spareroom door. "Someone must be ill in there. I'd best see to this quickly." He jerked open the door.

Martitia dropped the dishcloth she was holding. Her face turned white. As though drawn by a magnet, she hurried across the floor to the spareroom door. Behind her she heard Eunice and Ruth continue to clatter the dishes without pause. In front of her the girl saw the spare bedroom stretch neatly in its accustomed immaculate plainness.

But on the two double four-poster beds were stretched four unaccustomed figures. The four outstretched forms were large and masculine. They were unmistakably Jonathan, Milton, Barzillai, and Addison. Martitia gasped. Jonathan, Milton, Barzillai, and Addison were writhing and moaning in apparent agony. The covers of the four-posters had been neatly folded back. Four pairs of enormous, copper-toed shoes reposed neatly on the floor by the beds. The four boys writhed and doubled and moaned under the plain white homespun canopies on the bed tops. Martitia cried out.

Dr. David bent toward Jonathan and Milton. He examined their rolling eyeballs, poked their heaving stomachs. From Milton and Jonathan he hurried on to Barzillai and Addison. His ruddy face showed grim in the sunlight through the plain homespun curtains. Martitia found herself wringing her hands.

Only Clarkson stood upright by himself over near the wall. He said nothing, just stood silently watching Martitia in the doorway. Over his shining black head a framed piece of needle-point spelled out in cross-stitch "God Is Love."

The four boys on the beds writhed and moaned louder than ever. A weak cracked voice from one of the beds spoke agonizedly: "Pa, do you think we'll die? Are we poisoned by something we et at dinner?" The tones of the cracked voice bore a faint resemblance to Barzillai's usual vigorous baritone.

Dr. David felt Barzillai's pulse and put a hand on his forehead.

"Oh, we're poisoned, we're poisoned," moaned a powerful bass voice from the other bed. "We're poisoned by something we et at dinner." Jonathan's tones were despairing.

Martitia twisted her hands like a dishcloth. Dr. David worked his hands up and down on Barzillai's chest. Clarkson stood and looked at Martitia. Martitia stared at the four pitiful figures on the beds. She put her hands over her face finally and broke out into weeping.

At sound of her tears one of the prostrate forms stirred. The moaning of the form increased. The prostrate form's voice announced in a strong bass: "It must have been *Martitia's bread* that poisoned us! It must have been Martitia's bread! We're going to die of Martitia's bread!"

Like a dreadful chant three other voices joined the bass moan. The spare bedroom reverberated with four voices chanting in unison: *"We're going to die of Martitia's bread!"*

The girl took her hands from her wet cheeks. She stared into the room with drowned blue eyes. Suddenly a brickdust red swept from chin to temples of her slim face. She looked at Clarkson over by the wall. Clarkson's black eyes dropped before her glance. His curved mouth drooped downward. Clarkson stared at his shoes. Martitia turned toward Dr. David. Dr. David twinkled back at her with unwavering mischief in his softly shining eyes.

Four figures rose from the canopied beds, chanting: *"We're going to die of Martitia's bread!"*

Without a word Martitia turned and fled from the doorway. She hesitated not a second in the kitchen where Eunice and Ruth still washed the dishes. She made for the front door onto the porch.

Eunice's strong voice echoed after her: "Thee will have to get used to the teasing of the Gardner menfolk, Martitia. They mean no ill. They are good men. 'Twas so that David teased me when first I was married to him. 'Tis haply good for the soul of sober folk like thee and me to be teased. Thee will get used to it as young Eunice Gardner did."

Eunice's words echoed in Martitia's head as the girl hurried down the path toward the springhouse: "Thee will have to get used to the teasing of the Gardner menfolk." Where the blackheart cherry trees spread their branches over the path she climbed awkwardly up into one wide-spreading low tree. Around her the leaves were dense. She put her head against the smooth trunk of the cherry tree and let go her tears. She cried loudly, as a child cries, not bothering to wipe away the wetness from her face. Her tears spattered on the satiny bark of the cherry tree.

From below a voice suddenly spoke her name. Martitia brushed the water from her lashes. There was Clarkson close to her. His head reached level with the crotch of the cherry tree where Martitia crouched. Clarkson peered at her through the leaves. Then he drew himself adroitly up and joined the girl in the tree. He settled his sturdily built frame in a fork of two branches. Then he looked at her.

"I came to say I'm sorry for what we did, Martitia. I'm truly sorry. 'Twas mean to tease you so. Your bread"—he hesitated redly—"your bread was beautiful bread. Don't pay any mind to our teasing. If you'll only stop caring we'll do it no more. It's because you mind so dreadfully we keep on making you miserable. Will you forgive me for my share in the nonsense? 'Twasn't even clever nonsense, only foolish and more than a little cruel. I'm sorry for my part."

Martitia sniffed noisily. She brushed water from her cheeks with grimy hands.

Clarkson grinned. "You have smudges of dirt on your face. I'll try to wipe them away." He leaned over and wiped her face with a cherry leaf.

Martitia wavered into a smile.

Clarkson wheedled: "Pa bade me go to the woodland and leave the salt for the sheep before I knocked off work today. Will you go with me? I promise not once will I tease you or be mean to you. You have my word on it. And any Gardner's word is better than a bond." His open, handsome face was earnest.

Martitia hesitated. She searched his brilliant black eyes, his generous lips. He shook back the tousled shock of his black hair.

"Please come, Martitia."

"All right. I'll come."

They climbed down from the cherry tree. Clarkson picked up the salt sack where he had left it on the grass under the tree. They set off together through the midday stillness and heat.

"We're going to the wood's plot where Pa keeps the log for the sheep's salt," explained the boy.

"What sort of a log?" Martitia looked puzzled.

"You'll see when we get there."

"Does Doctor David have a great many sheep?"

"Enough for the wool cloth and for mutton. Pa uses the extra fleeces in barter. There may be two hundred sheep. Nobody knows for sure each year. It's only now and then, when my sheep collie, Sandy, and I bring up the sheep for some special reason, that they can be counted. And then maybe many of them are missing. Sheep stray pretty far sometimes."

"Don't you keep the sheep in barns like cows?"

Clarkson grinned. "No, Pa marks the sheep and turns them out in the woods. They roam and feed themselves most of the year. Everybody's flock has liberty to roam without hindrance."

"Don't the sheep eat up other folks' crops?"

"You're very ignorant, Martitia." Clarkson's smile belied the harshness of his words. "Farmers fence in their fields for crops. The sheep can't get at them often. Do you want I should tell you how we manage the sheep?"

"Yes." The girl sounded very meek.

"In April, after the lambing time, the sheep are all sheared. The lambs are marked. Then the flock is turned out into the woods. Salt is left for them in the salt log.

Except for that, no other attention is paid them till autumn. Some folks shear again then. But Pa only shears a few strong sheep that weren't found in April. Now and then Sandy and I round up the sheep so's Pa can select a ewe for the table meat. In winter, when there's deep snow or when a wolf comes about, we bring up all the sheep to the rail sheds behind the hay barn."

Martitia pondered these matters silently. The two young people walked on companionably. The boy kept brambles from tearing Martitia's dress. Her face began to show a clear pink. Her drooping mouth turned up.

Clarkson whistled a tune. "I should have brought Sandy along. Sandy's a fine sheep dog. I tied him up for fear you'd be nervous. You're such a scary little girl. All of us boys think our own special dog is best. Jonathan's dog is a pointer. Milton and Barzillai have setters. Addison's dog is a hound. We like to go hunting for wild turkeys and rabbits and ducks. Pa had a sheep dog bigger than Sandy. But it died in May. Pa loves dogs. He'll get him another. Even the fierce dogs love Pa. I think he could train a wolf."

Martitia's face looked meditative. They came to the woodland plot. It was surrounded by dense trees and shrubs, forming a good windbreak for the sheep in bad weather. Tufts of sheep's wool hung on bushes here and there. Clarkson showed Martitia a long, hollow log with round holes cut along the side.

"The sheep stick their noses through the holes and get the salt. Sheep never take too much. At least Pa's Merinos don't."

"What are Merinos?"

"They're the best sheep for wool. Pa's full-blood Merino three-year-olds give nigh onto five pounds of wool to the head. It takes a pound and a half of wool, well washed, to make each yard of woolen cloth that Louisa weaves on her loom." Clarkson paused, with a puzzled look on his face. "Land knows who will do the weaving now that Louisa's gone."

"Well, anyway, you can still eat mutton."

"Yes, but we need the wool cloth to cover our backs with in winter. Of course Pa can use the extra fleeces in barter for Jonathan's and Milton's schooling this winter when they go away. Wool's worth forty cents a pound now."

"Where are Jonathan and Milton going to school?"

"Milton's going to Doctor Madison Lindsay's medical school near by at Jamestown. He aims to be a physician like Pa. Jonathan's going far off to Orange County to Mr. Bingham's school."

"What sort of schooling will Jonathan get in Orange County?"

"Jonathan will study classics at Mr. Bingham's school for two years. Then he aims to read law with Pa's old friend, Judge Debow, at his home in Orange County. Jonathan's the smart one, Martitia. He's read law books since he was a little boy. He'll go to the Legislature in Raleigh someday." Clarkson spoke proudly.

Martitia said nothing. Clarkson suddenly caught her sleeve. "There come some sheep to get their salt. Stand with me at the side of the wood's plot. We'll watch them."

They stood at the edge of the clearing and looked at the salt log. Three ewes approached the log. Three black noses disappeared into the round holes. The sheep licked contentedly.

Martitia exclaimed in disappointment: "But the sheep are all gray and dirty. I thought they'd be snow-white."

Clarkson looked down at the sunshine glinting in Martitia's solemn blue eyes. "Thee is so ignorant, Martitia. So ignorant and so little and so scary. But thee is a pretty thing to have about the place. Thy face is dirty, too, like the sheep's wool. Come, let us go home and wash thy black little face."

He turned her gently about and started her toward home. The afternoon sun was all about them.

CHAPTER VI

A Letter from Richmond

I T WAS THE FIRST DAY of September when Martitia's letter came. Dr. David stood in the door of his office, built in a separate small building at the right of the main house, and handed Martitia the folded paper with its blob of red sealing wax.

"Here is your long-awaited letter, child. It was for this I sent Ruth to call you from your noon butter-making. I was here doctoring a patient when Stephen Starbuck brought the letter from Jamestown. Stephen required twenty-five cents due on two sheets instead of one. That means your aunt Margaret has written you a long epistle."

Martitia's face lighted. Her eyes burned. "Before I take the letter I'll go fetch the sum to pay you. I have more than forty dollars of my father's in currency."

"Keep your savings, child. Don't try to pay me."

But Martitia ran and fetched the twenty-five cents before she would take the cherished letter. Then she ran up to her room. Her hands were shaking. What would

the letter say? Would Aunt Margaret have her? Or would
Aunt Margaret not have her?

She broke the red seal. The two sheets fell apart.
Martitia's breath caught as she began to read.

Richmond, Virginia
10th August, 1831

My dear Martitia,

*Your news grieved me deeply. Your mother was my be-
lovèd sister. I am sad at her passing. I never reconciled myself,
though, to her marrying your father. Neither did her own
father and mother, my parents, throughout their lives, recon-
cile themselves to the marriage either. Yet death levels all
differences. Your mother was so beautiful and so gentle. She
had great strength under her softness too. No one could ever
reason her out of marrying your father.*

*Your father did not equal a Peyton in blood. He never
knew how to make money either. Yet I must put the thought of
that behind me, now that he has passed on.*

*You ask if you may come to live with me and your uncle
James. It is true that your coming will crowd your delicate
cousins so that Letitia and Evelina will have to give up their
separate rooms and sleep together to their discomfort. But
your uncle James and I feel that a Peyton should not lack for
protection and upkeep. Your uncle James will, therefore, make
you his ward and will administer your father's small estate at
Asheborough. You may come to us. Your uncle James cannot, of
course, be expected by even the most critical onlooker to leave
his business and fetch you here. You must travel to Richmond
alone. Although you are young, you can contrive to take care
of yourself on the long journey by stage. This Dr. David
Gardner is doubtless an uncouth country fellow, but he may*

know how to place you under the care of some respectable lady also traveling by the coaches to Richmond. Your uncle James says that if you have forty dollars, he need send you nothing for your trip. Your funds will suffice. The coach fare is ten cents the mile. Your uncle James says that in the wilds of Carolina the stages achieve but five miles an hour. So do you bestir yourself to set out. It is not fitting for a Peyton to be beholden further to common Quakers.

You will be glad, I know, to leave those uncouth country folk. Your uncle James says to convey to this Dr. Gardner his briefest thanks for befriending you. If the fellow is too much a yokel to understand the niceties of well-born folk, do you offer him a few dollars in payment of your upkeep. We shall look to see you in due season.

Your loyal aunt,
MARGARET PEYTON RANDOLPH

Martitia's eyes traced the last words. She broke out into excited tears. She clapped both hands together.

Then she read the letter once more. She came to the words: "You will be glad, I know, to leave those uncouth country folk." A shadow darkened her face. Her mouth began to quiver. Her chin puckered. All light went out of her countenance.

Suddenly Martitia dropped the letter to the floor and put her head over in her hands.

Leave Eunice? Leave Dr. David? Leave Clarkson and the blackheart cherry trees? Never go down the stairs again and see Grandfather Daniel sitting by the kitchen window? Never again make butter in the springhouse or set light bread to rise on the hearth? Never wash her face again under the morning-glory vine or watch the sheep eat salt from the salt log in the woodland plot? Never again, forever, see Jonathan stand on his head on the back porch in the early morning sunlight?

Martitia followed her letter to the floor. She pressed her face against the cool oak boards. She made a heap of blue homespun there. Above, around, below, the hip-roofed house gave back its noonday serenity. Somewhere a horn blew. Presently there floated up a sound of laughter, large and masculine. Those dreadful boys were home again!

The girl sprang up and tried to erase the signs of her tears. She hurried down the steps to the kitchen. Everyone was eating and talking by the time she got there. As she entered the door everyone stopped talking. Confusion showed on the faces around the red-checked cloth. Only Grandfather Daniel went placidly on eating and drinking. Martitia took her place by Dr. David. The conversation resumed awkwardly. Martitia could scarcely swallow the chicken and dumplings on her plate. Once she looked up and found Clarkson's black eyes staring at her. He flushed and looked away quickly.

Grandfather Daniel ate on till he had finished his pear cobbler for dessert. Then the unquenchably curious old eyes turned in Martitia's direction. The far-away old voice broke the clatter of spoons and dishes. "Thee has received thy letter from thy aunt in Richmond, Martitia. Son David says that Stephen Starbuck brought it over this noon. What did thy aunt say? Is thee to go to her in Richmond to live?"

Martitia saw all eyes turn in her direction. She answered in a small, faint voice: "Aunt Margaret says I am welcome to come and live with her and Uncle James and my cousins in Richmond. She bade me ask Doctor David to find a respectable lady traveling by the stagecoach to Virginia to take me in charge at once. Uncle James cannot leave his silver business to come and fetch me."

"If I had so precious a responsibility as thy uncle James I would not tarry to come to fetch my own niece myself, business or no business," said Grandfather Daniel. "Haply thy uncle James is a man of small ancestry, unlike us Nantucket Gardners. Thy uncle James serves Mammon."

Martitia rose. She mumbled confusedly: "I must go begin my packing." She turned to Eunice. "I will come back presently, Aunt Eunice, and help redd up the kitchen." She fled.

Behind her she could hear a jumble of voices break out in the kitchen.

Upstairs in her room she inspected her letter once more, for the third time. The hands that handled the letter moved as if with distaste. Martitia turned darkly red when she came to the passage: "Your uncle James says to convey to this Dr. Gardner his briefest thanks for befriending you. If the fellow is too much a yokel to understand the niceties of well-born folk, do you offer him a few dollars in payment of your upkeep."

The girl clenched both hands till the letter was crumpled up. She cast the crushed sheets to the floor and stamped upon them.

Call Dr. David a yokel! Dr. David who had taken her from the dying arms of her mother and father and had offered her compassion and tenderness and protection! Pay Dr. David a few dollars in return for her upkeep! Dr. David who had not even wanted Martitia's twenty-five cents' postage for Aunt Margaret's own letter!

"No," decided Martitia, "Aunt Margaret has not changed. She will never change. There in her fine house in Richmond she still sits and looks down her nose at all the rest of the world except Peytons and Randolphs. There she will always sit, she and Uncle James and the five cousins who are as bright and cool as the silver that Uncle James handles in his business."

Martitia gave the pages on the floor another stamp. She opened the door and went back downstairs. In the kitchen door she stood transfixed. Around the table still sat Dr. David, the five boys, Eunice, and Grandfather Daniel. Only Ruth had left. Dr. David drummed one big hand on the table. Jonathan had his chair tilted forward. Clarkson leaned over the table, finishing an earnest sentence. He broke off as Martitia entered. To see six great, able-bodied men sitting idle at noonday! Would the marvels of this day never cease?

Martitia addressed herself to Eunice: "I am ready to help redd up, Aunt Eunice."

Dr. David rose. "I have something to say to you, Martitia. Your aunt Eunice will spare you from helping today. Come over with me to my office while I grind some powders for Jeremiah Macy's bilious fever."

Martitia followed Dr. David outside and over to the little office where he received his patients. The Quaker picked up his mortar and pestle from the table. "While I grind the powders, child, do you sit down there and listen to me. By now you have learned that country Quakers cannot stop work to enter into long conversation. Without the evils of black slavery a Friend must work hard with his own hands."

Martitia sat down. For a while there was silence in the

little house except for the grinding sound of the mortar and pestle. Then Dr. David spoke:

"Do you love your aunt Margaret, Martitia?"

Martitia turned red. She answered, after hesitation, very low: "Aunt Margaret was never very kind to my mother, it seemed to me. And she looked down on my father. Aunt Margaret is very elegant, but Aunt Margaret is not a person one loves. It is kind of her, though, to take me to live with her when I am left alone. It would be very ill-hearted of me if I did not feel grateful to her."

"Feeling grateful is not the same thing as loving, child. Do you love your uncle James and your cousins?"

Martitia drooped her head. "Please do not ask me that. Ask me instead whether they love me. I do not think they do. My mother and father lived across the town from them for all the time since my mother married my father until we moved to Asheborough four months ago. Yet we only saw them perhaps twice a year. Is that a sign of love? My uncle James's house is fine and elegant. He owns many slaves. My father's house was small, and he had no money to buy slaves with. My uncle James and his children like elegant houses and elegant people. They do not care very much, I think, for me."

"Would you rather live with people who loved you, even though their house was not a fine one, than to live in an elegant house with little of love or none, Martitia?" Dr. David's voice sounded deliberate and grave.

Martitia looked wonderingly at him. "Yes sir. But 'tisn't for me to choose."

Dr. David paused in his pounding of mortar with pestle. For a while he stared out the window. Then in a quiet voice he began: "Yes, child. It *is* for you to choose. Would you rather live with your uncle James in his fine house in Richmond or would you rather live with us Gardners here at Centre in our simple home in Guilford County?"

Martitia saw the whole room tilt before her eyes. For a second everything turned black. Then the walls returned to their normal four-square white. She stared back at Dr. David with agonized hope in her face.

"You can't mean, sir, you'd let me stay on to live with you here forever in Guilford County?"

"The choice is for you to make, child. My home and the home of Eunice is your home, too, if you choose to make it so."

Suddenly Martitia could see only a great blur where Dr. David had been before. She blinked wildly. "But you said, sir, would I rather live with people who loved me than with those who didn't. It couldn't be, sir, that you and Aunt Eunice *love* me!"

"It is so, Martitia. You are a good little girl, better maybe than you know. If you were our own brother's child Eunice and I could not have learned to value you more. My wife Eunice is not one to give affection where affection is not earned. It is Eunice herself who first proposed that we urge you to stay here with us at Centre."

Martitia put her head over.

Dr. David went on softly: "As for me, child, there would be a little empty spot inside me, like the empty chair at my left hand at table, if you went away now."

Martitia began to weep.

Dr. David left his mortar and pestle and came over to

her chair. He put an enormous hand on her dark hair. "Does thee want to stay with us, child? Is that what thy tears mean?"

At his soft Quaker speech, directed toward her for the first time, Martitia could only nod her head in speechless acceptance.

He went back to his grinding of powders. Presently Martitia lifted her wet face. She flushed over her difficult words. "But what do the boys say about my staying on, sir? They dislike me dreadfully. I'm sure they won't want me to become one of them."

Dr. David's whole face wreathed itself in a giant twinkle. "Hasn't thee found out about those boys yet, Martitia? Hasn't thee learned that menfolk don't tease except where there's affection to prompt it? 'Twas that rascal Clarkson himself who spoke the first yea to his mother's wish to keep thee here."

Martitia reddened more deeply. She went on very slowly: "Does your son Jonathan say he wishes me to stay also?"

"Jonathan is not one to do overmuch talking, child. Let Jonathan be. He said naught *against* thy staying at any rate, save to warn me that I must straightway notify the County Court of the presence here of an orphan."

Martitia continued after a pause: "And does Ruth wish me to stay on also?"

Dr. David hesitated. He answered firmly: "Ruth will be glad of thy help with the butter and the ironing and the dishes."

Martitia straightened her shoulders. "Doctor David, if I stay with you here instead of going to Aunt Margaret in Richmond I must learn to be as useful as Ruth is. I must learn to be as useful as your daughter Louisa was before she left. I could not take your care and offer less than a real daughter would offer in return. If I cannot learn to be as useful as a real Gardner, then I must go to my own kin in Richmond."

Dr. David glowed. He reached over once more and patted Martitia's head. "Did I not say that thee was a good little girl?"

Then, with a sudden return to his normal language, Dr. David began to speak in practical terms. "You can be as useful as Louisa was to us if you wish. You can become the weaver for the family. It is a sorely needed task for us Gardners. 'Twas ever Louisa who wove the woolen cloth and homespun and jean to clothe us Gardners with. Since she has married and gone with her William to Indiana my wife Eunice has her hands too full with household tasks to include the regular weaving also. In a few months Ruth will go back to her schooling at the old-field school. She can scarce do much weaving in her spare time. Being the family weaver is a full-size job, worth a daughter's whole service. Would you like to be that one of the Gardner daughters who manages the weaving?"

The girl's whole self glowed with joyful response. "To be one of the Gardner daughters I would work my fingers to the bone. I have finished my own schooling now. If Aunt Eunice will but teach me how to handle the loom I will stay at it night and day. Only try me a while, and witness that I speak the truth. I am somewhat lazy, but I will overcome my laziness. I promise you that with all my heart and soul."

The big Quaker sifted his powders into little packets.

"My wife Eunice says you have a gift of housewifery in your small hands. You have mastered quickly the making of good bread and sweet butter. I look to see you master well the intricacies of weaving. But there will be hard and discouraging days ahead for you in the learning. Weaving is a far more difficult job than bread-making. You will need infinite patience and tenacity to achieve good, evenly woven woolen cloth and homespun and jean."

"Only try me and I will prove that I can stick at a task when once I have undertaken it."

"You will remember, child, that all of this matter of your staying with us Gardners is subject to the will and permission of your aunt Margaret and your uncle James. It must be for them to say whether you may become one of us or not. Obedience to the commands of those in family authority must ever be the first duty of a young person. I would not counsel you to rebellion or ingratitude. Do you go now at once and write to your aunt Margaret and beg her permission to stay with us. I will myself write to your uncle James in regard to the legal matter of my becoming your guardian. We will pray that the still, small voice of the Spirit will speak to their hearts and suffer them to give their family consent."

Martitia rose with alacrity. "I will go at once and ask leave of Jonathan to use his quill and ink. I have one more sheet of letter tissue. I will write to Aunt Margaret immediately."

"It is most probable that Jonathan has already returned to the fields. The sun is long past two o'clock."

"If it be so, then I will write the letter with his help tonight."

The girl hurried over to the main dwelling. Eunice met her in the shining kitchen with a grave smile. She pointed to the table. "Son Jonathan left his quill and ink and sealing wax there on the table for thee to use if thee did wish it." Eunice took her small, compact form in its plain dark dress out of the kitchen and down the hill toward the springhouse.

Martitia surveyed the quill and ink. Meditatively she inspected the red sealing wax and the box of sand for drying the ink. Was the owner of that ink so eager for her to leave Centre that he had left the ink and quill on purpose for her to use in telling Aunt Margaret when to expect her at Richmond? Or was the owner of that ink and quill so willing for her to stay at Centre that he had left the wherewithal for Martitia to beg Uncle James's permission to stay on forever in the hip-roofed house in Guilford County? Martitia wished she knew the answer to that unspoken question.

She got up at length and fetched her tissue letter paper from upstairs. Carefully she began her letter to Aunt Margaret. There was no tall, spare young man with hazel eyes and a wide, firm mouth to correct her spelling now.

> *Centre, North Carolina*
> *1st September, 1831*

DEAR AUNT MARGARET,

Thank you very much for saying I might come to live with you and Uncle James and my cousins. I am grateful to both of you. I know my mother would be glad, if she could know.

But since I wrote to you, a great priveledge has been offered me. Dr. David Gardner has requested me to stay here

in Guilford County and live with him and his family al-
ways. I wish excedeingly to stay. They love me. And I love
them. Dr. David says I can become like his daughter. I will do
the weaving for the family in place of Louisa Gardner, who
has married and gone to Indianny to live. Will you and
Uncle James give me your permisshun to remane here?

You need have no fear for my future. The Gardners are
fine folks. They are Quakers, as I told you. Dr. David is not a
strict Quaker like his wife, Aunt Eunice. But he and his
children are birthright Quakers. Except that they don't use
plain language all of the time, they are good Friends. None of
them has ever been disowned from Meeting. Doctor David's
father told me so. And they are not backwoods yokels, like you
said. They are well educated, and they are people of fine blood.
They came from Nantuckit. They are all good skolars, even
the females. Dr. David has five big sons. Clarkson is the
kindest and the most handsume. Jonathan is the cleverest one.
I am afraid of Jonathan.

Please write that I have yours and Uncle James's permis-
shun to stay here at Centre. I send my love to Letitia and
Evelina. Dr. David is also writing to Uncle James.

Your grateful neice
MARTITA HOWLAND

CHAPTER VII

Warp and Weft

MARTITIA CLIMBED the ladder to the attic room over the springhouse. Eunice went ahead of her. The attic room looked as it had looked the day that Ruth had first shown it to Martitia on her initial morning at Centre. The red peppers still hung from the rafters; still the window at the front looked out on the poplar tree; under the window the brazier still sat on the floor. Martitia surveyed the hand loom intently.

She spoke to Eunice: "From this day forward I'm going to spend a great deal of time in this room handling the loom. I hope I will learn to weave quickly, so as not to take too much of your time instructing me."

"Thee must learn patience, Martitia. Weaving is a tiresome task. Is thee certain thee wouldn't rather take over some of the cooking or ironing instead? That would free me for the weaving once more myself, as before Louisa was old enough to undertake the job."

"No, I wish to be the weaver. I wish to take Louisa's whole place. Otherwise how could I earn a daughter's

78

right to eat and drink and sleep in the Gardners' home?
Do you believe, Aunt Eunice, that my aunt Margaret
and my uncle James will let me stay on here with you in
North Carolina?"

Eunice smiled gravely. "Did I not counsel thee to learn
patience, child? Thee is as quick and impatient as the
blackbirds out yonder in the treetops. 'Twas only yesterday
thee wrote thy letter to thy aunt Margaret. 'Twas only this
morn that David took thy sealed sheet and his own missive for thy uncle James over to Stephen Starbuck's house
for carriage to Jamestown and the coach there. 'Twill be
many a week before thee has thy answer. Or David his.
Learn to be patient, Martitia."

The girl made a rueful sound. "You bid me learn
patience, ma'am. Your son Jonathan bade me learn to
laugh. There seems to be a great deal for an ignorant girl
such as I am to learn in this world."

"Let us begin with the weaving first. Assuredly that
will teach thee patience. Thee can learn the laughter
from David and the boys."

Martitia stood close to the loom. She inspected it as
Eunice talked. It looked to her rather like a bed frame
with an open top where a canopy should be but where no
canopy was. She spoke quickly: "The loom must be half
again as long as Jonathan is tall. It is nearly as wide as I
am tall."

"Thee needn't guess the height, Martitia. The loom
measures six feet from the floor, foursquare and true.
David fashioned it himself from the best, sound, solid
pine, free from knots and shakes. The mortises are perfectly adjusted. The loom will not bend or spring or
shake when used. 'Tis a good loom."

Martitia inspected the parts of the loom interestedly as Eunice pointed out their uses. Eunice showed her the threads of the warp already stretched by Louisa down the center of the loom like innumerable strings of a violin. The little Quaker woman sat down in the weaver's seat and demonstrated to Martitia how to place her feet on the treadles to open the warp, lifting the threads so that the shuttle with the weft thread could be thrown through by hand.

Adroitly Eunice swung the batten to beat the lines of weft thread together. As her feet moved on the treadles, the harness above that controlled the warp threads rose and fell. Into the successive openings in the warp Eunice's quick fingers would throw the shuttle with the weft from right to left and back again. With the comb of the batten she would beat the threads of the weft together.

A thin line of woolen cloth began to show across the warp of the loom.

Martitia clapped her hands. "It looks very easy. Let me try it now, Aunt Eunice."

Eunice looked at her gravely. "The ease is not in the loom. 'Tis in the hands and feet that ply the warp and weft. Thee can try now. But first let me give thee some facts to remember. 'Tis not the amount of the cloth, but the quality that counts. There's no excuse for bad weaving. The weaver should aim at absolute perfection in his webs. Thee will learn character as well as cloth-weaving if thee does the job well and patiently. The watchfulness, taste, and skill thee must learn on the loom will stand thee in good stead in thine own web of life also. Remember that."

The girl answered soberly: "I will remember, Aunt Eunice."

Eunice left the weaver's seat. She yielded the narrow plank to Martitia. Valiantly Martitia settled herself. She pushed her feet on the treadles. She held the threaded shuttle ready for use in her right hand.

Up flew the harness with the warp. Martitia awkwardly threw the shuttle with the weft through the opening. She swung the batten. A snapping sound from the loom caused Martitia to stop in dismay.

"But I did as you did, Aunt Eunice. What is wrong?"

"Thee made the opening for the passage of the shuttle too large. That strained thy warp threads till they of necessity broke. We must find and join the right ends together at once."

Painstakingly Eunice showed Martitia how to go through the intricate task of mending her warp threads. Perspiration began to gather on Martitia's hot temples. She sighed at the tedium of finding and tying and tensing the threads again. It was a long time before she was ready to continue her weaving.

She pressed the treadles once more at last. She lifted her warp. With slow wariness she regulated the opening this time. Through the warp she carefully threw her weft shuttle. She allowed the batten to swing forward evenly and press the weft straight. A neat line of woven threads appeared on the loom.

Martitia cried out in triumph: "I've woven a whole neat line all by myself!"

Eunice smiled. "Pride goeth before a fall. Have care, Martitia. Remember to go slow."

Martitia put all her soul into the next line of weaving. She pressed the treadles, threw the shuttle, swung the batten. Another neat line of woven threads appeared. The girl began to hum a little tune. She repeated the process several times without hitch. Then she stopped abruptly and leaned over her web. The width of the woven cloth was decreasing slightly in size. It drew inward.

Martitia turned red and looked helplessly toward Eunice. "What have I done wrong now?"

"Thee has drawn thy weft thread too tight with the shuttle. Let thy hand be more careful in adjusting the tension."

The girl sighed wearily. "There seem to be many things that can go wrong with a web in the weaving, Aunt Eunice."

"Yea, many things. As with the web of life itself. But thee will learn to avoid thy difficulties and failures in both if thee determines on patience and perseverance. Let thy lesson be done for this day. Tomorrow we will come again and try once more. We will come every day till the task is learned. Thee will slowly master what is necessary. Later on thee must learn also to master the warping board for preparation of the weaving. And thee must learn to spin the thread also. There is much for these small hands to instruct themselves in. Does thee still wish to be the Gardners' weaving daughter?"

Martitia wiped beads of perspiration from her forehead. She answered steadfastly: "I still wish to be the Gardners' weaving daughter."

"Then so be it. Come, child, let us go up to the house and prepare food for the noonday dinner. A Gardner daughter may well help prepare food for her Gardner menfolk."

Martitia glowed. Was she not being accepted into the

charmed circle of the Gardners of Nantucket and Guilford County?

On the way up the hill Eunice spoke quietly. "By another month Ruth and Addison go back to the old-field school. Another daughter will be invaluable to me then without Ruth here all the day. And when Jonathan and Milton have gone to their respective institutes in Hillsborough and Jamestown, David will need thee to cheer him of his loneliness. David loves well and deeply his boys. David is a family man."

"When will Jonathan and Milton go away, ma'am?"

"In one more week the house will be quieter than ever it was before. Jonathan and Milton leave together on next Fifth Day."

Martitia missed a step in her upward climb.

At dinner she stole occasional glances at Jonathan and Milton. One week was not very long! Of course there'd be Clarkson still, and Barzillai, and Addison. Ruth too. But no Jonathan and no Milton!

After the meal was finished and the work done Martitia retired down the hill to the cherry trees. She climbed up in the branches of one and settled her small self in the crotch. The sun was warm, even though September was here. The leaves were still dense about her. She sat with a solemn look on her grave face. Presently, what with the heat and a heavy dinner, she began to look sleepy. She nodded a little in comfortable melancholy. All of a sudden she drooped her head against the safe tree trunk and dozed.

She woke with a start to hear voices below, somewhere near. They were masculine voices. The girl listened with startled wonder on her face.

A bass voice was speaking. "Sit down in a ring, all of you. It won't be long now till we'll be scattered to the four corners of the wind. It's time to take stock of ourselves and make some pledges to each other."

Martitia remembered that it was Saturday afternoon. No work for the boys. This accounted for Jonathan's voice sounding here in the yard near the cherry tree. She looked uncomfortable at her unwitting eavesdropping. Would it be better to stir loudly and let Jonathan know she was here? No, he would only laugh at her and make her miserable somehow. Best to stay still till he went away. Who else was with him? She hadn't long to wait for an answer.

Clarkson's warm tenor echoed Jonathan's voice: "Yes, let's sit on the ground in a ring, all of us Gardners."

Jonathan's bass broke in again: "Addison, you sit next to Barzillai. Milton and Clarkson, you fill out the circle."

There was a rustling sound below in the grass. Then silence.

Jonathan's voice spoke at last, gravely, slowly: "In one week we five Gardner brothers will be parting for the first time. Life will bring us new problems and new experiences. Shades of difference might arise between us if we are not careful. We must determine in advance that no dissension shall ever insinuate itself into our brotherly relations. If this world should destroy everything else worth living for let it not mar what has been our chief happiness heretofore: the genuine brotherhood of the Gardners."

Martitia listened breathlessly to hear what would come next.

Barzillai's steady baritone broke the stillness hesitantly,

as though he were thinking aloud with difficulty. "I feel and have long felt that we have been a favored family. I have often thought that we have lived for each other and in each other's affections more than is usual for brothers to do. The thought would be a happy one to me that we might live as a band of unbrokenly loyal brothers here in this world and meet again in an unbroken band in the next."

With wondering ears Martitia heard Clarkson's tenor take up the slow thread. "I know it isn't thought fitting for men, especially Friends, to tell their affection for each other. But I'm not ashamed to say I love my Gardner brothers. If so be any of you ever needs me I'd give my life for any of you gladly. You'd do the same for me."

From her hiding-place in the cherry tree Martitia caught the awkward assent of four masculine voices.

She put her hand over her lips to keep back the exclamation of unbelief that nearly disclosed her hiding-place in the tree crotch. Those amazing boys! Had they always hidden under their laughing, uproarious exteriors this core of grave, strong tenderness? Was it possible that laughter like theirs was a product of strength, not foolishness? She caught her lip to still its trembling.

She heard Milton say slowly: "If any man ever says evil of one of us brothers to another let us stop the words in his teeth. There is nothing in the history of our family in which each of us has felt so much pride as in the uninterrupted fraternal feeling which we've held since childhood."

"No man shall ever come between us," said Addison in his boyish voice.

"And no one of us shall ever let his own selfish heart

come between his brother and himself." Jonathan's words fell like awkward blows into the still afternoon.

Martitia suddenly buried her head in her skirts. She stuck her fingers in her ears. No one had a right to hear the stark confession of five strong men who believed themselves alone. Laughter might be listened to. Not heartbeats!

When she took her fingers from her ears a long time later her eardrums registered only birdsong and leaf movement. The boys were gone.

For several minutes she waited, still. No one must see her come from the cherry tree and up the hill. She must creep down to the springhouse and climb the hill at the side of the house. By the back way she might enter unnoticed and get to her own room without discovery.

The girl had much to think on as she climbed the hill at the side of the hip-roofed house. Might it be, after all, that laughter came strongest from the lips of those who felt gravest underneath? Might it be that she, Martitia Howland, did not feel more deeply than others felt just because her lips were grave? Might it be that she, like young Eunice Gardner, could learn to laugh fine laughter from the lips of the strong Gardner men? A laughter which was all the larger for the strength of the grave hearts that beat underneath.

CHAPTER VIII

Oh, What a Tangled Web!

JONATHAN AND MILTON went away on horseback next Fifth Day. Jonathan headed toward far-off Hillsborough and Milton toward near-by Jamestown. Their dogs went with them. The house on the hill settled down to autumn routine. Red and yellow colored the oak trees and poplars. Leaves started dropping from the blackheart cherry trees. The men on the farm were busy outdoors. Martitia saw little of them.

Every day but First Day she climbed the ladder to the attic over the springhouse. Eunice went with her as teacher and guide. Little by little Martitia accustomed herself to handling the loom. Eunice seemed not to believe in overmuch praise. Martitia treasured her infrequent approving nod.

One day in early October Eunice spoke to Martitia after breakfast. "This day Ruth will be thy teacher. There is work here at the house with the candle molds that none but myself may do."

Martitia stared at Ruth and sighed.

The two girls set off together down the hill. Martitia felt somewhat like a small blue butterfly accompanying a large brown bumblebee. The trees overhead spread colored branches. The wind spoke a word of coming frost.

Martitia turned to Ruth breathlessly: "The poplars and hickory-nut trees get ready for winter so shiningly. The earth's a big loom today where some giant is weaving colored cloth."

"Pretty is as pretty does. The leaves on the hickory-nut trees may look handsome. But I'm more concerned with the nuts underneath. Hard and brown they are, but they're a deal more useful than the gaudy leaves."

"Is nothing worth having that isn't useful? Isn't it enough for some things to be just pretty without having any use?"

"I don't think so. I mind me when I was a child I learned better than that. Being a girl on a farm, with work to do, I learned not to set any store by mere prettiness. There was always a useful thing that needed doing. I'd hate to see a child of mine grow up to value pretty things like you do, Martitia."

" 'Twould empty the world dreadfully to take away all the pretty and leave just the useful, Ruth. Folks like me just naturally cherish pretty things. Maybe you'll have a child or a grandchild who'll love pretty things in spite of yourself."

" 'Tisn't likely." Ruth turned smartly into the springhouse and climbed the ladder.

Martitia followed reluctantly. She settled herself to do the day's weaving at the loom. Ruth stood and watched her grimly.

Yesterday, with Eunice there, Martitia had found the

weaving easy. Today, under Ruth's dour glance, every-thing seemed to go wrong. She worked the harness im-perfectly. Her openings of the warp did not prove clear. Instead of the gentle, throwing motion of the shuttle which she had achieved by hard effort she found herself throwing and catching the shuttle awkwardly. She left the weft thread too loose in the shed. Her cloth began to show loops and kinks.

Ruth surveyed her coldly. She offered no help.

Defiantly at last Martitia sought to retrieve herself. She threw the shuttle violently through the shed. Snap went several of the warp threads.

For a second she started to fling the shuttle to the floor and run away from those grimly appraising eyes. In time she caught herself. She set to work in silence to repair the broken threads. Her fingers were all thumbs.

Ruth spoke at last sharply: "It seems to take this particular tub a long time to stand on its own bottom. I thought you had learned to make better cloth by now, Martitia. Do you want that I should give you simple instructions like a mere child?"

"No, I can get along without directions. When I'm done mending these threads I'll progress all right."

Martitia continued to bungle on with the broken threads. At last she set to weaving again. She worked doggedly. Presently she knew that something was going dreadfully wrong with the web. But what it was she could not figure. Ruth volunteered no help. Martitia set her lips firmly and continued weaving. At length her web looked entirely hopeless. She got up from the wooden seat.

"I reckon it's nearly noon. It's best I stop for today."

Ruth spoke wryly: "If you had thought fit to ask me, I could have told you what was wrong with the weaving. You should have wound the already woven cloth onto the roller in order to keep the batten in its proper position. That was all that was wrong. Why didn't you ask me for advice?"

"Every tub ought to stand on its own bottom," said Martitia wildly.

She made for the square opening and rushed down the ladder in a whirl of petticoats. She did not wait at all for Ruth. Up the hill she ran at full speed. Into the kitchen she burst. She looked for Grandfather Daniel over at the window. He was not there. Eunice came from the back porch.

Martitia addressed her in a rush of words: "Please, Aunt Eunice, where is Grandfather Daniel? I want to talk to him."

"David's father is lying down on his bed. David's father begins to tire easily of late. David says that the old man's age is beginning to tell on him. Go talk to him in his room, child. He says thee brings light with thee when thee comes into a room."

Martitia ran into the hall and knocked at Grandfather Daniel's door. The old voice answered her dimly. She went in. It was the first time that she had ever been there. It struck the girl immediately as resembling the pictures she had seen of ships' cabins. The two windows were small and round, shaped like portholes. The bed was built into the wall of the room like the bunk on a ship. A whaler's chest stood in one corner. The floor was bare and shipshape.

Grandfather Daniel spoke from his bunk: "Come

closer, child. My sight is getting dimmer than once. Thee is welcome to Grandfather Daniel's cabin whatever be the reason for thy unaccustomed visit. The old whaler is feeling less seaworthy of late."

Martitia came close. She slid down on the floor without a word. She buried her face in the bedspread on Grandfather Daniel's bed.

The old man's hand crept out and stroked the dark hair awkwardly. "Don't thee cry, child. Tell Grandfather Daniel what ails thee. Didn't I tell thee once that naught was worth crying about? Soon the present is all past. Tell Grandfather Daniel about thy woes."

Martitia's voice muffled itself in the bedspread. "Oh sir, I am so miserable. Your granddaughter, Ruth, hates me. She has no wish or will for me to stay here and be a Gardner daughter. I must go and live with my uncle James in Richmond."

"So that is what ails thy pretty little head? It is Ruth, is it? Well, thee has come to the right man to smooth away thy trouble. I can tell thee a story that will make thee understand my granddaughter, Ruth. It is a story that goes back ninety-two years, to the Island of Nantucket, off Massachusetts.

"Once a little boy was born on the Island of Nantucket, in the year 1739. His name was Daniel Gardner. His father, Joseph, was a sea captain, a Friend, who owned a whaling schooner. His mother, Lydia, was a Friend also. Little Daniel was a very solemn boy. He grew up to be a solemn man and became a solemn sea captain. But happily for that solemn Daniel he married a laughing girl named Eunice Hussey. And Eunice Hussey bore him a great laughing son with black hair and black eyes. That son's name was David." Grandfather Daniel paused a while.

He went on presently: "And when David married another Eunice in his turn he passed on his laughter to each one of his twelve children but one. That one child was named Ruth. Ruth inherited the solemn heart of her grandfather. So Ruth grew up to be a solemn girl."

Grandfather Daniel stroked Martitia's dark hair wistfully. "Don't thee be afeared of Ruth and me, Martitia. We have no laughter like the rest of the Gardners. We have no prettiness and softness like thine. Someday thee will learn to laugh like my son David and his boys. Ruth and I can never learn. We must always be sober schooners sailing our stubborn, seaworthy ways. But thee must not be afeared of us. Underneath our barnacles we bear good hearts."

The girl lifted her head and stared at Grandfather Daniel with a light gathering over her face. "Then Ruth does not hate me, truly? I was never afeared of *you*, sir. I'll try not to be afeared of Ruth."

The old man stroked her hand fumblingly. "The old whaler is too tired to talk longer. Go now and wash the tears from thy gentle little face. Ruth does not hate thee. She only has no way to be gentle or gay or soft, as thee can be. Go now, child; but come again to the captain's cabin whenever thee wishes. Thee is welcome. I'll make thee my second mate if thee has a mind to go to sea with old Daniel Gardner."

Martitia went away. She looked thoughtful the rest of the day. Whenever Ruth was about Martitia sprang to help her with unaccustomed speed. She studied Ruth's sharply pronounced features in wistful silence.

Twilight came to the house at last. The boys and Dr. David trooped in to supper. The fire in the long kitchen gleamed bright. The pewter spoons and jugs shone merrily. As she helped Eunice and Ruth to dish up supper Martitia found the blaze on the hearth did not feel unpleasant to her face and back. A small chill of autumn came at sundown now in Guilford County. Was not tomorrow the eighth day of October?

Martitia settled at Dr. David's left hand. The candles on the table flickered softly. The Gardners all bowed their heads in silent grace-before-meat.

When Martitia lifted her head after grace she found Clarkson's black eyes shining at her across the table. "Tomorrow the few selected sheep that we missed last spring are to be sheared, Martitia. Do you want to come out to the barn and watch Pa and Barzillai and Addison and me do the shearing? If Pa should be called away to doctor a patient maybe he'd let you take a hand in his stead."

Dr. David broke into a laugh. He surveyed Eunice wickedly. "If I am called to physic a patient, Eunice, while I'm shearing the sheep, you can go doctor the case in my stead."

He turned to Martitia. "Your aunt Eunice is a better doctor than I am. Patients only take me when your aunt Eunice is not to be had."

Eunice's lips quirked.

Clarkson spoke insistently across the table once more: "Will you come out and watch us shear the sheep tomorrow, Martitia?"

Martitia looked at Eunice. "May I leave the weaving tomorrow, ma'am?"

"Thee can leave the weaving. Thee deserves a rest."

"Then I will come with you tomorrow and watch the sheep being sheared, Clarkson."

Clarkson glowed.

CHAPTER IX

Uncle James's Reply

"**P**A IS READY to do the shearing now, Martitia. Are you ready to come watch?" Clarkson stuck his black head through the door from the back porch into the kitchen next morning. His collie, Sandy, was at his heels.

Martitia hung her dishtowel neatly on its nail. She turned to Eunice with an eager face. "Is it all right that I go now?"

Eunice paused in her meat-grinding and nodded briskly. Ruth, busy in the corner of the kitchen, snorted aloud: " 'Tis a waste of time to stand idly watching the sheep lose their fleeces. Wasted time can't be earned again. When I go back to school next week you'll wish you had this wasted time back again."

Martitia fled out into the October sunshine where Clarkson waited. The weather had turned warm again since yesterday. The back yard and the pastures and the fields looked almost asleep in their nine o'clock serenity.

The sky above was a deep blue. Lazy clouds floated there. Clarkson and Martitia walked across the back yard under the late gold of the poplar leaves. Sandy followed them.

They came to the icehouse, with its boarded-up square pit in the ground. Over the pit was a shingle roof reaching from the ground on each side to the comb.

"Let's stop long enough to slide down the roof of the icehouse once," said Clarkson. "I dare you to try it."

The girl hesitated. "I'd have to take off my shoes. Unless I were in stocking feet I'd never be able to get to the top of the comb."

"Sit down on the grass. I'll take off your shoes."

Martitia sat down. She stuck out her black shoes. Her blue homespun skirt lay like a fan on the grass in front of her. The boy knelt down and unlaced the small copper-toed boots. Gravely he tickled the bottoms of Martitia's helpless stocking feet.

Martitia wriggled her toes and screamed. Clarkson held on to the toes. He continued to tickle, all the time keeping a comically solemn countenance.

The girl moaned in anguish: "Oh, Clarkson, Clarkson! Just when I think you're to be trusted not to tease me you do it all over again. Let go my toes! Let go my *toes!*" Her voice rose in a miserable crescendo.

Clarkson let go of the toes. He surveyed Martitia. He beamed angelically. He lifted his fine tenor voice in a ridiculous chant, openly impromptu:

> *"There's a lady goes*
> *In stocking toes.*
> *She's got blue eyes*
> *And a button nose."*

Martitia stopped screaming and put her hand to her short nose. "I *haven't* got a button nose!"

"Yes, you have. I like button noses, though." He looked at Martitia. "I like button noses and short dark hair tied back by a blue ribbon. Why do you wear your hair short like that instead of long like other girls?"

"When I was twelve I had a dreadful fever. My hair was longer than to my waist then. I tossed so with the fever that my hair got fearsomely tangled. My father had to cut it halfway to my shoulders to get the tangles out afterward when I was well. My mother said that short hair became me, since my head is small. So ever afterward she wished it cut so."

Clarkson rose from the grass. He held out his hand. "Come, let's run up the roof of the icehouse and slide down. It'll be no fair if you touch hands to the shingles."

Martitia hopped up. She hesitated only a second. Then she lifted her long skirts, took a running start, and sped up the side of the icehouse on her stocking feet. She reached the comb without touching a hand to the shingles. Then she tucked her skirts about her, sat down, and slid to the ground on the other side, using her unfortified homespun seat for cushion.

Clarkson followed her example, disregarding utterly the risk of splinters to his legs in their blue-jean trousers. When both of them had reached the grassy ground in a swift rush on the other side the boy turned to Martitia.

"I never thought you'd do it. But you did it! You've come a long way since that first afternoon when you climbed out of Pa's gig in front of our house last July."

The girl smiled. "Maybe I'll even learn to laugh at last, instead of holler, when you boys tease me."

Clarkson began to sing noisily:

> *"There's a lady goes*
> *In stocking toes.*
> *She's got blue eyes*
> *And a button nose.*
> *But* when *she will laugh*
> *Nobody knows."*

The collie, Sandy, lay on the grass by them. Suddenly Sandy barked. Martitia and Clarkson looked up. A head with a pair of large ears appeared around the side of the icehouse. The ears wiggled. Then Addison himself appeared, in full, from around the side of the roof. He addressed Clarkson disgustedly:

"So this is the way you go to fetch Martitia, is it? Pa's getting tired of waiting for you. He told me to come fetch you on the instant. It's getting late."

The boy and girl rose hurriedly. Martitia retrieved her shoes. The three young people started off toward the hay barn. At the entrance to the barn Martitia saw a small yard had been penned off. Ten or twelve sheep, snow-white in the sun, were standing there on clean straw.

"These are the sheep, all washed and dried, to be sheared. 'Twould be cruel to shear many in the fall. But these few strong sheep we missed in April can spare their coats. The weather is going to be mild till November or December."

Martitia went with Clarkson and Addison into the barn. Dr. David and Barzillai waited there. Dr. David spoke briefly: "You were a long time, Son. But I don't know that I blame you." He smiled at Martitia.

"Let's get started, Pa," said Barzillai.

Martitia watched the men from a vantage point at the side of the big hay barn. Addison, Clarkson, and Dr. David ranged themselves at three long tables in the center of the barn floor. Barzillai went outside. He came back bearing a sheep, and delivered it to Dr. David. Dr. David placed the sheep on its back on the table, holding it strongly but gently till it stopped struggling. He grasped his shears and commenced cutting the wool. Adroitly he cut, changing the animal from side to side, or changing the position of his own knee to hold the sheep in place on the low table.

Martitia watched him, lost in wonder at the speed and skill and intricacy of the task. By now she saw that Barzillai had given to Clarkson and Addison each a sheep also. The boys cut and twisted and turned almost as skillfully as their father did. Painstakingly from each sheep was sheared an entire unbroken fleece. In between shearings Barzillai cleared the tables and took away the fleeces for tying. Martitia grew so absorbed in watching that she lost all sense of time.

Ruth appeared suddenly in the door of the barn. "Pa, you're wanted up at the house. Stephen Starbuck has brought you a letter from Jamestown. He wants you should pay him the postage on it."

Dr. David handed over his sheep to Barzillai for finishing. He wiped his hands. "You boys finish alone. I'll go up and tend to Stephen Starbuck's money." He went away with Ruth.

Clarkson spoke to Martitia: "You look like a lamb with a blue ribbon around its neck. Are you tired?"

"No, it's fine to see the silky fleeces come off like woolen jackets."

"It won't be long till noon. We'll stop working then. One morning's watching is enough for you."

At dinnertime, when the horn blew, the boys and Martitia went up to the house. Dr. David came in from his office across the yard. He looked preoccupied, unlike his usual gusty self. He did not smile once at the boys' nonsense during dinner. Martitia had a feeling of unease. She could not enjoy her meal.

As soon as it was over Dr. David got up and beckoned to Martitia. "Come with me, child, out on the porch. I want to talk to you."

Martitia obediently followed. Dr. David pointed to the October world outside. "We'll walk a spell down the road. There are times when a man has need of the open heavens to compass his thoughts. This is one of those times. There are no sets of walls large enough to hold a man's thoughts when he has been stirred to anger almost past the endurance required of a true member of the company of Friends."

Dr. David strode down the steps. Martitia set her feet to follow wherever his long stride directed. They set off down the road. For a while the big man seemed lost in thought. He spoke finally with a great effort at control:

"Child, the matter on which I must speak concerns your uncle James."

Martitia grew white.

"I have had a letter from your uncle James."

Martitia swallowed hard. "Does my uncle James say I must come to him and Aunt Margaret in Richmond? Is *that* what he says?"

Dr. David answered wryly: "Your uncle James seems under the impression that the only thing which has hin-

dered your coming already to Richmond is the greedi-
ness of a rough country yokel in North Carolina named
David Gardner."

Martitia gasped.

Dr. David went on: "A man brought up in the faith of
Friends may not indulge in long indignation however
just. Nor may he righteously form hasty conclusions.
There is good inherent in every man's soul. If I but learn
how to appeal to the nobility in your uncle James there
will be a response. But until that time comes, your uncle
James has tried my spirit and my temper nigh to the
breaking point. I am but a man as well as a Friend, and a
man of strong will and strong blood."

The girl held her breath.

For a long minute Dr. David paused. His words fell
more soberly afterward. "Your uncle James has too hastily formed a conclusion. He has concluded that a rough
Quaker fellow in North Carolina named David Gardner
saw in the helpless need of a bereft orphan a way to make
himself some of this world's goods. In short, your uncle
James professes to believe that if I had not known you to
possess a small piece of property in Asheborough I would
have long since sent you safely packing by the coach to
Virginia. In wishing to keep you here as my ward your
uncle James believes that I plan to share in what small
rents might come to you from Asheborough."

Every trace of color drained from Martitia's lips. She
broke out fiercely: "Oh, *sir!* . . ."

The big Quaker put out his hand and closed the girl's
lips. "Do not speak, child. Such calumnies should be met
with silence. I remember how my mother, Eunice Hussey,
bade me as a little angry boy to answer naught to the jeers

of the other lads who were not Friends when they taunted me with my determination not to fight back at them. The hardest thing a Friend has to do in this world is to keep silence and to stay his tongue and his hand from violence. You are not a Friend; but while you bide with us of that company, here at Centre, do you follow our gentle faith and precepts."

Martitia looked ashamed.

Dr. David spoke in his gentlest voice: "Thee is a dear daughter, Martitia. I need not tell thee how thy uncle James's words are wrong."

The girl's whole ardent spirit flamed into her eyes as she looked wordlessly up at him.

He patted her hand. "Have no fear. Thy uncle James is not thy true uncle in spirit. He has forfeited his right to tell thee what thee is to do or where thee is to dwell. Thee may stay with us here at Centre if the courts of Guilford will give me thy guardianship."

"Could my uncle James *make* me come to him and to my aunt Margaret in Virginia, Doctor David?"

"The laws of North Carolina governing orphans are not so clear to me as they would be to my son Jonathan if he were here now. It may be that thy uncle James has best legal rights as nearest of male kin. I do not know. But haply thy uncle James will have satisfied his sense of family pride in demanding thy return. He may let the matter rest there. 'Tis unfair to misjudge thy uncle. He is fulfilling his family duty as well as his family pride."

Martitia looked relieved.

Dr. David chuckled for the first time. "We will try our habit of Friends' silence upon thy uncle James. If aught more is to be said against thy staying here it must be said by Mr. James Randolph, not by us. I shall write to Jonathan in the meantime for further knowledge about thy guardianship. Jonathan had thought to handle the matter of thy guardianship in June when he returned from Hillsborough. The courts of Guilford are in no hurry. But now we must write to Jonathan for directions. He will tell us what to do."

Martitia's eyes shone. "Jonathan will know all the laws. Is not he to become a lawyer? Clarkson says that Jonathan will someday go to the Legislature of North Carolina and help fashion new laws."

Dr. David inspected Martitia closely. He said nothing. He turned her about in the road and started her toward home.

She sighed after a while. "Till Jonathan himself comes home in June I shall be afeared that Uncle James will do something by law to make me come to Richmond. Uncle James is proud. He does not like to be crossed in his will. He might contrive to send someone to fetch me to Virginia."

"That danger we will face if we must. But Jonathan will know a way to circumvent thy prideful uncle James Randolph. Be of good courage, Martitia. Jonathan will come home in June. And all will be well then."

CHAPTER X

Winter Comes to Guilford

C LARKSON WAS RIGHT in foretelling that the
weather would stay mild through October and November at Centre. Each morning as Ruth and Addison set
off for the old-field school they scarcely had to wear jackets at all. Martitia, left behind at home, found the mild
autumn days fuller than ever of work. Eunice turned more
and more to the little Virginia girl for a daughter's help.
Martitia took over the feeding of Eunice's flock of wild
turkeys besides her weaving. Eunice counted on the extra
turkeys to be used in barter. Martitia grew accustomed to
seeing scant actual currency in this North Carolina country district.

One evening during the very beginning of December
the Gardner family was gathered about the kitchen fire
after supper. Addison and Ruth, close to the candlelight,
bent their heads over school chores of arithmetic sums

and English-grammar rules. Clarkson sat on the floor by the hearth cracking hickory nuts with a stone. Eunice was setting the light bread to rise. Barzillai mended a shoe. Dr. David talked desultorily to Grandfather Daniel as they both shelled corn. Martitia sat watching Clarkson.

Suddenly Clarkson raised his head from the hickory nuts. "Pa, when we were all at the tanyard today Reuben told me of his visit to Wilmington. Reuben aims to go back down to Wilmington next summer and be apprenticed to his uncle Jethro there. His uncle Jethro owns a wholesale grocery business in Wilmington. Do you think you'd ever be willing to let me go to Wilmington and get a job in Jethro Swain's warehouses?"

Dr. David surveyed his son. "Every man must receive the light from within. If the Spirit bids you go to Wilmington to enter Jethro Swain's grocery warehouse, then go you must. But I'm free to say it would be a sore trial to have you go so far away."

Martitia looked forlorn in the firelight.

Clarkson spoke again animatedly: "Reuben says that Wilmington is a fine city. And the river harbor there is full of schooners from the Indies and other ports. Barzillai as well listened to Reuben's tales. Didn't you, Barzillai? Tell Pa what marvelous words Reuben had to say of Wilmington and his uncle Jethro's warehouses full of sugar kegs and kegs of rum and salt and turpentine."

Barzillai lowered the mended shoe sole. "Yes, Pa. They were fine tales that Reuben told. A man could make himself a fortune quickly in wholesale groceries on the Cape Fear at Wilmington. The whole Atlantic Ocean would be his delivery medium. I've a mind to go to Wilmington, too, and make a fortune in sugar and salt and turpentine. But not in rum. Rum's evil."

Martitia listened for Dr. David's reply. She covered her face with one hand, as though the fire felt too hot. The reply was a long time in coming.

"I'll have to think on these matters of Indian schooners and fortunes made in kegs of turpentine and salt. You boys couldn't go till summertime in any case. I'll have to look into these matters with Reuben's father. Christian Swain has a level head for more than the running of a tanyard. In the meantime there's needful work to be done here on the farm."

Martitia let her breath go out in a little sighing sound. For a while, at any rate, Clarkson would not be gone.

Grandfather Daniel spoke suddenly. "Has thee made up thy mind, David, about securing Christian Swain's Spanish sheep dog? Didn't thee say the cur dogs were continuing to infest our flock till thee needed another larger, stronger sheep dog?"

"Yes, Pa. The cur dogs are continuing to infest the flock. They've killed several of our Gardner sheep. I need a stronger dog, and a fiercer one, than Clarkson's sheep collie. When I was at the tanyard today I inspected Christian's Spanish dog. He is an evil-looking fellow, large and powerful and ugly-tempered. He smells of wolf. Christian says it's likely that the animal is half or a quarter wolf in very fact. Christian had to take the dog in barter from the innkeeper near Jamestown who owed him for saddles and harness. That dog might prove valuable to us. I took a strange fancy to him."

Clarkson broke in excitedly: "Reuben showed all of us the dog, Grandfather Daniel. While Christian mended

Pa's saddle Reuben took Pa and Barzillai and me out to inspect the Spanish dog. The dog's name is Vigilante. He came from Spain, probably in company of Spanish sheep. A traveling Spaniard who died at the inn near Jamestown had the dog with him. It was left unclaimed. The dog's so fierce-tempered that everyone is afraid of him. Reuben says that that dog is strong enough to kill a man or a wolf as quick as a cur."

Martitia spoke frightenedly: "Such a dog might be a danger as well as a protection."

Dr. David reassured her: "I've a hand with dogs, Martitia. I'd keep him chained, if necessary, till he grows accustomed to us and to the Gardner flock if I settle in my mind to secure him. I've a thought to take him from Christian. Christian will accept wool or new corn in exchange."

The matter dropped there for the evening. Everyone went to bed. But Martitia kept in her mind the story of Vigilante, the Spanish sheep dog, and of Jethro Swain's warehouses in Wilmington.

The matter of the warehouses did not come up again for some time. But two days later Dr. David appeared in the back yard leading a great dog by a chain. He unloosed the dog and called to Eunice and Martitia in the kitchen:

"Do you both come out and observe the fine points of Vigilante and be introduced to him. He is undoubtedly an evil-looking animal, yet he has a nobility about him that stirs my soul."

Martitia timidly followed Eunice into the yard. The Quaker woman strode forward fearlessly to the dog. For a minute it looked as though the great animal meant to spring upon her. But whether from Dr. David's hand upon

his bristling neck hairs or whether from a strange recogni-
tion of equal courage in the dauntless little woman con-
fronting him, Vigilante neither sprang nor bit with his
bared teeth.

Martitia from a safe distance examined Vigilante curiously. He was a tall, flat-chested, flat-sided dog with a
long back and narrow loin. His neck and forelegs and
thigh indicated great strength. His head was small. His
coat hung about him in thick, loose folds. His eyes were
what frightened Martitia most. Those eyes were small
and bloodshot, set close together, giving the face a sinis-
ter, wolfish look. Martitia shivered.

Dr. David laughed aloud at the girl's frightened face.
"Come and be introduced, child. Unless you be a cur dog
and attack the Gardner sheep you need not fear Vigilante. He will not hurt you. He has not the affectionate
nature of Clarkson's collie, but I tell you there is great
character in this dog's countenance and bearing. Give
him a few weeks to become accustomed to us Gardners
and to our Gardner sheep and you will see that Vigilante
is a valued member of the family."

Martitia came closer, but she still stood a little behind
Eunice. Vigilante surveyed her. Then Eunice set a strong,
light hand on the great animal's matted hair. Vigilante
growled, but he did not seem angered. Proudly reserved he
looked, thought Martitia, yet somehow not actively quar-
relsome. A more evil countenance she thought she had
never seen on an animal before.

Martitia watched respectfully as Dr. David and Vigilante went away toward the stock barn. The dog strode
forward, never breaking his long, loping, shambling trot.
His heavy bushy tail almost trailed on the ground.

When the boys came in from work they were openly enthusiastic over Vigilante. Clarkson, with his vivid face alight, instructed Sandy in future friendship to the newcomer. All three boys set themselves to see that Vigilante became domesticated to the Gardners and the Gardner sheep and the Gardner dogs.

Martitia, for days, heard the echoes of their masculine enthusiasm over Vigilante mingling with Dr. David's. She heard their stories of how Vigilante adopted the Gardner flock along with Sandy. As for Dr. David himself, it appeared that Vigilante after one necessary flogging gave the whole of the passionate heart under his evil-looking exterior to his new master. And soon it seemed to Martitia that all the cur dogs in the neighborhood must have been killed, according to the stories related by the Gardner men.

Christmas crept upon the Virginia girl. Milton came home from Jamestown. But Jonathan was too far away to make the trip. The Gardners held a serene but sober festival for the Christ child. It was quiet in the house on the hill. Martitia longed for the old noisy Christmases with her mother and father. Tears seemed often to mount close to her lids.

The new year brought heavy snows to Centre. It took all of Martitia's courage to keep going down to the springhouse for even a brief stint of weaving each day. The little attic room was cold. The few coals she had in the brazier did little good. Martitia could spend less and less time at her loom. Life was hard for the city girl.

One morning soon after New Year's she threw off her blankets with a sigh in the cold little room of hers under the roof of the Gardners'. Ice coated the windowpanes.

She dashed into her heavy wool clothes and fairly threw herself down the stairs. Into the kitchen she whirled. Her nose smelled buckwheat cakes in Eunice's warm, fragrant kitchen. Martitia forgave the world its winter frost.

Clarkson surveyed Martitia from the breakfast table where the other Gardners were already seated. "The cold has made your cheeks look like magnum bonum apples, Martitia."

"Clarkson is getting to be a poet," teased Addison.

Clarkson grinned back sunnily at his brother. "Well, if you'd rather, I'll say that Martitia's cheeks are like sheep's noses.

Martitia felt her cheeks. "My cheeks aren't dirty, Clarkson. Sheep's noses are black."

Addison got up and turned a somersault. "You'll kill me yet, Martitia. Don't you know that the kind of sheep's noses Clarkson is talking about are nice little red apples shaped like the ends of sheep's muzzles?"

Martitia looked confused.

Clarkson adroitly changed the subject: "Pa, the almanac says the next few weeks are going to be extra cold. Hadn't we best bring up the sheep to the rail sheds? They'll need fodder and shelter."

Dr. David paused in a giant mouthful of buckwheat cakes. "I'll take Vigilante and round up the flock tomorrow, Son. Today I must tend sick folks. My saddlebags are full at the door now. There's lung fever among the slaves over at the Armfield plantation."

"Can't I stay home from school and round up the sheep?" begged Addison.

"No, Son."

"Can't I stay home and go over to the pond to see if the ice is thick enough to be cut yet for the icehouse?"

Dr. David looked at his youngest son with twinkling eyes. "Seems to me you're powerful anxious to be useful today, Son. Is that a sign that William Reynolds is having a spelling bee at school today?"

"Now, Pa." Addison pretended to be aggrieved. "I just don't want you to forget about the ice-cutting."

Dr. David rose. "Well, Son, you're right about it's being time to cut the ice from the pond. You can take a holiday from school one day next week and we'll go for the ice. I'm off now for the Armfield place."

True to his word, Dr. David let Addison stay home from school on the following Thursday to cut the ice. Martitia, duly excused by Eunice from her tasks, elected to go too. Only Ruth insisted stolidly on her accustomed school-going.

Eunice started the family out on Thursday morning with a mighty breakfast of porridge and pork sausages.

After breakfast Martitia stood in the kitchen, somewhat resembling a fat blue sausage herself in her many wrappings. She tied the last of her wool mufflers about her bundled-up neck. She tightened the strings on her padded blue hood. Clarkson and Addison and Barzillai came surging around her.

"We can't decide who's to take you on his wagon, Martitia," said Addison explosively. "You'll have to choose. Each of us boys will drive a wagon. We've borrowed two extra wagons from the Macys. Pa will go in one of those. Choose, Martitia."

Martitia swallowed hard. She turned pink. Clarkson's

dark eyes followed her intently. The girl brought forth a small, wavering voice: "I choose Clarkson."

Clarkson beamed.

A few minutes later Martitia and Clarkson drove along the frozen road in the front of a rattling wagon. The other wagons went ahead.

"How far is the pond, Clarkson?"

"About two miles, maybe less. Addison and I tested the ice yesterday. It's thick."

"How many trips will we make to fill the icehouse full?"

"At least three." Clarkson looked down at Martitia in her dark blue coat and hood. "I don't mind if we make a hundred trips with you along."

Martitia snuggled her chin deeper into her woolen collar. She said nothing. The horse's shoes made a ringing sound on the icy road. Clarkson began to sing in a jubilant voice to the quiet fields on either side of the road. His handsome face was ruddy with the frosty air. Martitia stared up at him admiringly.

Presently they reached the pond. Dr. David and Addison and Barzillai had already begun cutting blocks of ice from the frozen surface. Martitia got out and stood by the pond to watch them. The three boys and their father raced to see who would fill his wagon with ice blocks first. Fast and wildly flew the ice splinters. Dr. David rode off in triumph first. Addison came next. Then Barzillai. Then Clarkson and Martitia.

The homeward trip was a wild race. For the last half mile Clarkson stood up in the wagon, urging his horse on. Martitia screamed as the wagon lurched and jolted over ruts and stones. Back at the house, the wagons all lined up in the back yard by the icehouse.

With rapt interest Martitia watched the process of unloading and of packing the ice blocks into the empty pit in the ground. There was something mystically fascinating about that icehouse to Martitia. It was a boarded-up square pit about fifteen feet deep, with a vertical ladder dropping down the side of it into its dark mysterious depths. The square door, which Martitia knew was always kept securely locked, opened outward almost level with the ground.

There was a post to prop it by. Over the great door in the ground the shingle roof protected it from summer sunlight. Martitia remembered now how she and Clarkson had slid down that steep comb last October.

She got in everybody's way trying to see everything. Clarkson crammed ice down her back. She screamed and jumped up and down. Clarkson bellowed with joy. He spoke gayly to the girl as he came back from taking his last load down into the pit.

"Beware of the icehouse, Martitia, unless you've been a good little girl. There's ghosts down in there. It freezes a man's blood to stay down in the icehouse long, even in summer. But it's good for the health of a quarter of lamb or a side of beef in July."

"It's like shutting winter up in the ground and then taking it out to look at and handle in summer." Martitia's face glowed.

Addison, who had just come up, heard Martitia's words. He looked puzzled. "You do say the queerest fancies, Martitia. How can you shut up winter in the ground? Winter is time and weather, not something to shut up."

Clarkson looked at the girl with his dark eyes shining. "I know what you mean. It's a pretty thought."

Martitia regarded him gratefully. She climbed back into the wagon with him. They rattled back over the road to the pond for a second load. At the pond's edge they found that Dr. David had built a roaring fire with some logs. Martitia warmed herself at the fire while the wagons were being loaded. The flames reflected dully on the ice. Sometimes the smoke blew in a black, exciting cloud into her face. When the wagons were loaded Martitia and the boys and Dr. David ate the lunch that Eunice had packed in a basket for them. The food tasted marvelously good, mixed as it was with fire heat and pungent smoke and frosty air.

The two succeeding trips that afternoon to the pond and back seemed hardly less exciting than the morning ones to Martitia. She stood at last, near sundown, by Clarkson's side in the back yard of the house. They watched Dr. David stuff the great door to the icehouse pit with charcoal. Martitia saw the big Quaker seal the great door against future warmth by filling every crack with the charcoal stuffing. He lowered the door into place and locked it securely. Martitia felt a little shiver of fear at the great door's closing.

Clarkson spoke: "And now it won't be opened till summer. We've shut up winter in the ground." He touched Martitia's sleeve. "Come on. Let's run to the house and get warm. Pa and Addison are going to drive the Macys' wagons home. They'll come back on horseback. Barzillai's already gone to the barn with the other horses. Ma will have supper ready soon." He took the girl's small frosty hand into his large grasp. Snow had begun to fall.

"Hurry, Martitia."

The kitchen felt beautifully warm when they entered. Eunice nodded at them. Grandfather Daniel snoozed in his chair. They sat near the hearth to thaw themselves out. They talked in low tones. The fire crackled.

Presently Addison roared into the kitchen from the back porch. He fairly glittered with excitement. Hardly had he got the door open, bringing a burst of icy air with him, when he broke out in a thrilled voice:

"There's a *wolf* loose about Centre! Pa and I just heard the news when we took back the Macys' wagons. The wolf killed a young calf over at the Macys' pasture last night! Pa's going to set Vigilante to watching our sheep tonight."

CHAPTER XI

The Wolf

AT THE APPROACH OF TWILIGHT next day Clarkson came to Martitia where she was rolling out little sugar cookies for supper. "Don't you want to come out and watch Pa set Vigilante to the job of guarding the sheep from the wolf tonight, Martitia? That dog is almost human."

Martitia bundled up in her warmest wrappings and went with the excited boy. They crossed the back yard in the gathering dusk of approaching nightfall. Snow was thick on the ground. Snow had been falling all the night before and all the morning. After a brief let-up the fine, wind-blown flakes were falling once more. Martitia kept close to Clarkson in the eery world of dusk and swirling snow. A tiny circle of human companionship seemed to close them in, ringed around outside by endless wastes of snowy fields and lonely roads and gray twilight.

116

The girl shivered with an odd animal sense of something out of the ordinary, something tongueless and wild and forbidding. She broke into quick, breathless speech: "Do wolves attack humans, Clarkson?"

"Not often. Only when the human is about to attack them. Or when the wolf's close to starvation. This wolf probably came down from the mountains to find more food than is left up there. These rolling uplands are thick with cattle and sheep. But now that the word's out, there'll be little for him to get at. Every farmer will have rounded up his sheep and cattle and put them in shelter for the nights. Wolves don't attack in daylight. Wolves are gunpowder shy now. They're seldom ever seen. Only maybe once in a long while, when dusk comes on."

Martitia drew closer to Clarkson. She reached out her mittened hand and tucked it into the boy's arm.

Clarkson laughed gently. "You're a scary little thing, aren't you? Want to be scared some more by hearing how the Macys found their calf killed yesterday?"

In dreadful fascination the girl answered: "Yes."

"The Macys found a lot of blood where the calf was killed. It seemed that the wolf had torn open the calf's throat and had eaten till the head was off. The head was gone; they didn't know where. That calf's tripes were dragged a half mile away across Polecat Creek."

Martitia burst into tears. "Don't *tell* me any more. I can't bear it. The poor, poor calf!"

Clarkson patted Martitia's terrified shoulder. "I won't tell you any more. I'm sorry I scared you so. No harm will come to the Gardner sheep or cattle. The stock's all protected in barns. And just you watch how Pa sets Vigilante to guard those sheep."

The snow whirled about them. They came to the hay barn. Behind the hay barn were the rail sheds for the sheep. As they rounded the barn Martitia could see the sheds only dimly in the dusk and snow. But she knew from experience how Dr. David had formed them by placing poles close together and set into the ground with their upper ends resting on strong horizontal poles supported by crotched posts. How thickly the boys had stacked the pine boughs on top.

Inside their cozy half sheds now the sheep huddled together. From around the side of the barn came Dr. David with a swinging iron lantern. Barzillai and Addison were with him. The great dog Vigilante was at Dr. David's heels.

Dr. David roared to the newcomers: "We're just through tending the stock. Every living creature is under safe cover from that woods' vermin. Now we'll set Vigilante to guard the flock this whole night through. By next winter I aim to build a fence so tall about these rail sheds that not even a huge gray timber wolf could jump over it, let alone any lesser Carolina breed of the vermin."

Martitia shrank toward Clarkson as Vigilante came near. She never quite lost her sense of awed wonder at the great dog. He loomed tall and narrow and unapproachable in the dimness. Only his uncanny eyes glowed strangely in the flicker of Dr. David's lantern. Vigilante stood quiet, intently watching his master's every movement. Stupid and sleepy as that dog might appear all day Martitia had noted when she was about how nothing escaped his observation. Nothing seemed ever to be erased from his memory. In the dusk now he seemed to the girl like something out of an ancient legendary world. He was superb in his wild, reserved strength. Well she might believe that if he met a wolf single-handed there would be little doubt of the issue of that Gargantuan struggle.

"Now watch, Martitia!" Clarkson's voice in the girl's ear sounded hushed through the falling snow.

Dr. David paced in a great circle about the whole line of sheep sheds, Vigilante at his heels. Twice, three times, Dr. David traced his circle of footsteps about the huddled sheep in their half-open houses. Then he stood still.

For a second the great Spanish sheep dog hesitated. Then proudly alone he left Dr. David's side. He began to retrace in the dimness that circle of his master's footsteps about the sheep sheds. Slowly, like a sentinel, he traversed the guarded ring. Round and round that intangible circle went Vigilante in the dusk and swirling snow.

Dr. David broke into a proud exclamation. He turned to Martitia. "All night, till day comes, that animal will retrace my footsteps about the sheep. I set him so to guard them last night. This morning he was still there, circling that ring. He'll permit neither man nor beast to pass in or out of that circle. We tried him with Reuben Swain this morning. Vigilante was like to be at Reuben's throat if I hadn't stopped him. And a ewe chose to stray out of the ring. Vigilante stopped her with a vengeance. I tell you, child, that animal is magnificent. He knows how to keep a trust."

Next morning Martitia remembered Dr. David's words when she started to do her morning's chores. It was increasingly difficult for her to keep her own trust. The bitter cold made work a real hardship. She listened gravely to Eunice after breakfast.

"When will thee be done with thy first length of true

woolen cloth at the loom, Martitia? Jonathan told in his letter yesterday how his old black suit is nigh worn through. I must cut and stitch a new suit of wool for Jonathan soon. Does thee think the dark blue cloth will be done this week? If so it be, then on Second Day of next week I can cut out Jonathan's suit."

"I can finish the cloth by the end of the week, ma'am. An hour each day will see the length ready to take from the roller." Martitia spoke determinedly.

Eunice looked at the girl consideringly. " 'Tis bitter cold this week. I don't know that thee shouldst weave at all till 'tis milder. Jonathan had better wait another month for his suit, I reckon."

Martitia spoke quickly. "I can make myself amply warm with thick clothes to do a mere hour of weaving each day, ma'am. I will wear three jackets and I will put on all my three pairs of wool stockings and my three wool petticoats. You'll see that I'm well protected. And I'll carry down coals for the brazier."

"Thee has surprising tenacity of purpose, child. I had not thought when first I saw thee that thy will was so strong under thy soft ways."

Martitia answered her earnestly: "Ma'am, if Vigilante can set himself to watch the sheep all night because 'tis his duty should I do less than endure a little cold in pursuit of my own trust?"

Eunice nodded slowly.

Martitia set off down the hill carrying a few live coals in a bucket for her brazier. She was thickly bundled and wore a pair of heavy wool stockings over her shoes for warmth. As she plodded through the snow she considered more than the frozen world about her. She shivered.

Had she undertaken more than she could fulfill in prom-
ising to finish the cloth for Jonathan's suit this week?

She thought fiercely to herself: "I would rather freeze
than not finish the cloth. And I would rather work my
hands to the bone than leave Centre and go to Uncle
James house where no one loves me."

Martitia sighed. She looked up at the frosted branches
of the cherry trees under which she passed. "Please, cherry
trees, don't let Uncle James send anyone to fetch me away
from North Carolina before Jonathan comes."

Next noon, as Martitia came back from her hour of
weaving, she found a ewe with its wool tangled in some
bushes near the snowy Dutch oven in the yard. She
hastened to tell Eunice about the ewe when she entered
the house.

Eunice reassured her: "David or the boys will fetch
the ewe back to the barn. It's easy to see how the ewe
could stray from the flock. David rode over to Centre on
a sick call. He took the Spanish dog with him. David
opined that no harm could come to the sheep in daylight."

Every day Dr. David and the boys discussed the wolf's
doings in great good humor. Barzillai was eager for the
bounty that would go to the killer of the animal. Addison
related bloody tales of previous wolves at Centre. Martitia
listened and shuddered.

At breakfast on Saturday, the last day of Martitia's
task of completing the woolen cloth, she listened nervously to the latest accounts of the wolf. Addison reported
that Reuben Swain had seen the animal at twilight, by
his barn, two days ago. The wolf stared at Reuben from
the shadows with glowing green eyes. Reuben vowed

that the wolf was big as a calf and gray. Barzillai related that the wolf had been seen by Samuel Macy. According to Samuel, the animal was black and not larger than a very large dog. Hezekiah Coltrane had told Clarkson that he saw the tracks of a wolf in his bottom land. The tracks measured five inches. Yet Thomas Bunker had reported to Dr. David measuring other wolf tracks and finding them only four inches long.

"But how can all these different descriptions suit the same wolf?" inquired Martitia of Dr. David.

"Man has a way of fitting reality to his wishes, child."

"One thing is certain, anyway," said Barzillai. "That wolf will have to kill or go hungry by daybreak tomorrow. He's made no reported kill for seven days. A wolf is said to be able to go for seven days on a full kill. That wolf must be hungry by now."

"There's a second thing certain," vowed Addison. "That wolf can't kill a Gardner sheep while Vigilante is here to watch them each night."

Dr. David interrupted the boys. He addressed Eunice: "Thomas Bunker told me yesterday that nine of my ewes had got folded with his flock in the rounding up. His sheds are crowded. He wishes me to come over today with my dog and bring the nine ewes home. I'll leave right after dinner. So I'll want my meal on the stroke of twelve."

Eunice nodded. After breakfast she set Martitia to molding candles.

"The long nights have made deep inroads into my candle stock. Thee can do thy weaving after dinnertime today. There'll be time aplenty then for thy one hour's stint."

Martitia molded candles all morning. At dinner she

watched Dr. David eat hurriedly. Afterward she saw him set out with Vigilante down the hill toward the spring-house. The short cut to Thomas Bunker's place led by the springhouse and in the direction of Polecat Creek. Dr. David promised to be back before nightfall with Vigi-lante and the nine ewes. He carried his gun.

Martitia went upstairs to put on her wraps. She was ready at last for her weaving. But as she passed Grand-father Daniel's open door the old man called out to her.

"Come into the old captain's chart room. Can't thee spare a moment's cheerful chatter to the old whaler?"

Martitia went into Grandfather Daniel's room. She moved reluctantly. Any other day or hour she would have welcomed the old man's invitation. But today she must go and finish her weaving! The winter days fled swiftly!

Grandfather Daniel began a long tale of Nantucket. The minutes slipped away. Martitia grew more and more uneasy. Finally she managed to direct the old man's mind into the channels of taking a nap. She fled upstairs and hustled into her heaviest wraps.

She was dismayed at the state of daylight when she emerged from the hip-roofed house. In an hour and a half, she reckoned, twilight would begin to fall. She would have to work swiftly to complete her cloth, take it from the roller, and be back at the house before night brought dimness in the grove and the fearful possibility of a flitting shadow peering with green, glowing eyes at her from the dusky trees as it had peered at Reuben Swain two days ago. In spite of Clarkson's reassurance that wolves did not attack humans unless attacked Martitia knew a gnawing wolf-terror in her heart. She scuttled along through the trees to the springhouse.

At the entrance to the springhouse Martitia stopped stock still. There, caught between two stumps near the door, was a ewe. The girl exclaimed in pity. Perhaps this was the same wayward ewe that had tangled its wool in the bushes by the Dutch oven five days ago. The ewe bleated weakly, gently, in cold and weariness. Martitia bent and strove to loosen it before she opened the springhouse door. She could not budge the ewe.

"Poor sheep. Don't be frightened. I'll finish my weaving. Then I'll go back to the house quickly and bid Clarkson come loose you and fetch you home."

The girl straightened. She went inside and climbed to the attic. Once in the cold little room, she went over to the window at the front and peered out. She could see the ewe below. The ewe huddled in the snow. It seemed comforting to Martitia to have something else alive and breathing and friendly near by in the lonely world of afternoon ice.

She put the hot coals from her bucket into the brazier. She set to work weaving. Her hands were stiff with the cold. She worked slowly. Determinedly she put her mind on the task of finishing the cloth at any cost. Her eyes told her first that it was growing dark. She hastily completed the last line of her warp in the waning light. She took the length from the roller. She fastened it into a bundle. Then she sanded the last flicker of coal in her brazier. She descended the ladder. Her trust had been fulfilled.

As her foot reached the last rung a sound from outside frosted every drop of her blood! That sound was the agonized bleating of the ewe. Even Martitia, city-bred as she was, could tell that that bleating meant stark terror unto the death!

The girl raced back up the ladder. She threw herself over to the window at the front. She leaned against the pane and stared out in a terror as frozen as the poor, doomed ewe below. The grove was growing gray. Under the trees had accumulated deep shadows. Under the poplar tree, across the path, Martitia saw two globes of moving light, unearthly and greenish in their color. A dark form outlined itself momentarily against the snowy hillside. Martitia stopped breathing. The dark form came nearer. The two spots of light grew larger. The bleating of the trapped ewe became heartbreaking.

Out in the open where the ewe was Martitia could see things plainly. It was only back in the shadows of the trees that it was truly dim. Martitia stifled a dreadful scream. The great shadow doubled on itself! The wolf was preparing to spring upon the trapped and desperately struggling ewe!

As the huge animal catapulted from the shadows of the poplar tree into the open Martitia saw a strange miracle take place. In mid-air that dark figure, before it reached the struggling ewe, was met by another dark form which seemed to hurl itself from the path that led up from the direction of Polecat Creek. The two dark figures intertwined in a gigantic struggle.

Frozen in awe at the majesty of that encounter, Martitia huddled at the window. In the lingering winter light she could see that the second dark animal was Vigilante. Fearlessly, titanically, the dog from Spain struggled to get his teeth into the throat of the wolf. Whatever moved in his wild heart in that moment Martitia could not know. She watched the two great figures twine and leap and roll, snarling, upon the ground. Her heart bowed in homage to the dauntless dog who would not give over his charge, the one poor ewe, into the teeth of that tremendous creature from the forests.

The girl could not tell how long the struggle lasted, nor could she even wonder in that stretched moment of agonized watching how Vigilante came to be there when the ewe needed him. She saw the wolf fall at last, roll in great contortions, and lie still. Above him, a moment, stood Vigilante in the dimness. Then the magnificent dog wavered and crumpled toward the ground.

Martitia saw Dr. David run forward suddenly from the path below. Dr. David, with his gun in his hands, ran forward and knelt by the dead wolf and the great living, bleeding dog.

Forgetting her own terror in pity, within a split second Martitia fumbled her way down the ladder from the attic still holding her bundle of woolen cloth. She ran over to the man and the dead wolf and the dog. The wolf was a dark, evil mass on the snow. Dr. David was examining the wounds of Vigilante. Martitia could see that the dog's throat was torn in a slashing gap. He was bleeding fearfully. No animal could bleed like that and live for long, she knew.

Dr. David dropped his head on the matted flank of Vigilante. He hesitated. He put his arms around the animal for a moment. Then he rose. "Stand back, Martitia. It's hard to get the flint to fire the lock."

The big man's voice was dreadful to hear though completely calm. Martitia stood back in the springhouse door and waited, knowing what must come.

A flash of fire broke the dimness. A shot rang out. Vigilante gave one swift movement. Then he lay still. Dr.

David stood in the clearing with his back to the girl. His shoulders shook. Beyond him in the path cowered a group of nine terrified ewes. The one trapped ewe in the clearing huddled silently between the stumps.

Martitia did not need to be told now how Vigilante and Dr. David had come to the ewe's aid. The short cut from Thomas Bunker's place led up this very hill by the springhouse door!

The girl put her hands to her face and broke out into heartbroken weeping.

CHAPTER XII

Grandfather Daniel

MARTITIA WENT ABOUT looking very grave the rest of January. She could not quite throw off her sense of tragic wonder at the death of the Spanish sheep dog. She determined to learn how to keep a trust as valiantly as he had. It was not till February thaws began to unfreeze the creek that she set her mind to pondering on other matters for more immediate worry.

No further word had come from Uncle James in Virginia. Dr. David, she knew by his own reassuring comments, had written to Jonathan for legal directions in preparing to meet any possible move of Uncle James's. But the big Quaker did not tell the Virginia girl what exact results had come of his correspondence. All Martitia knew was that when the proper time came Dr. David meant to apply to the court of Guilford for guardianship over her as an orphan.

The girl welcomed the milder late February days that foretold the approach of March. She could spend more hours at her weaving now. As March winds rattled the poplar tree outside the window of the springhouse attic she bent tirelessly over the loom and the warping board. April magic of raindrops and dogtooth violets could not lure her from her eager efforts at the webs.

By the advent of May even Ruth had to admit grudgingly that Martitia was becoming a fine weaver. The two girls sat together in the springhouse attic one early May morning. Ruth, free from school for the year, had mounted from her butter-making downstairs to chat with Martitia in unwonted frivolity.

"Your new pattern of cotton cloth is right pretty, Martitia. I'm glad you've left off the wool threads and have shifted the warp to cotton threads. We'll also need new blue jean soon. Addison's pants to his old suit are getting threadbare. Ma has already patched his seat twice. Jonathan wrote Ma that he particularly liked his new dark blue wool suit that Ma fashioned from your first length of true weaving. Jonathan will be home soon. He says Mr. Bingham's school will let out by May thirtieth. That should put Jonathan home on his horse by June fourth or earlier."

Martitia's face lighted. "June fourth is my birthday. I'll be seventeen the day that Jonathan comes home if he gets here that day."

"Jonathan will find you here if your uncle James hasn't sent a respectable lady to fetch you to Richmond with her by coach now that the weather is fine. Pa told Ma yesterday he was growing uneasy over your uncle James's long silence. Pa said that silence in any man but a Quaker is ominous. Pa thinks your uncle James is planning some sort of trouble for him and for you before Jonathan comes."

Martitia paled. She wet her lips. "I pray very hard every night that Uncle James will do nothing to try the issue till Jonathan comes. Jonathan will know the law and what to do about Uncle James."

"It's strange that your uncle James cares whether you come or stay, since he loses no love on you."

"Uncle James and Aunt Margaret think it's unfitting for a Peyton to be beholden to strangers."

"Your uncle James perhaps thinks the Gardners are humble folks who lack family pride of their own. To be a Randolph and to be wedded to a Peyton of Virginia is no whit finer than to be a Gardner from Nantucket, as Grandfather Daniel and Pa are." Ruth spoke harshly.

Martitia said nothing. Ruth went on after a pause. She sounded troubled. "Martitia, do you notice how Grandfather Daniel talks more and more of his boyhood on Nantucket? Do you notice how he almost never calls anyone a servant of Mammon any more? I'm afeared that Grandfather Daniel is losing his hold on living."

Martitia looked up. She surprised a softness on Ruth's face that she had never seen before. Martitia seemed to hear again an old voice saying: "Don't thee be afeared of Ruth and me. Underneath our barnacles we bear good hearts."

Assuredly some bond existed between the solemn old man in the house back yonder and this solemn young girl before her here today!

Martitia started to answer gently. But before she could speak a black head appeared in the hole where the ladder came up. A pair of black, laughing eyes came into view. Clarkson's whole sturdy, handsome self pulled itself up into the attic. He smiled sunnily at Martitia and his sister.

Ruth demanded sharply of her brother: "What are you doing away from the planting at this time of day?"

"I have Pa's permission to take Martitia walking to Centre with me. I've got to carry a message to the Swains. Ma opined that it was all right for Martitia to leave her weaving."

Martitia got up quickly. The sunshine through the window had already teased her fancy. The poplar tree showed green, new leaves. A bee buzzed in the red peppers overhead among the rafters. Ruth snorted her way downstairs to the abandoned butter-making.

Martitia and Clarkson set out by the road to Centre. The boy seemed unusually gay even for a Gardner. He sang loudly to the fields on either side of the road. Dogwood trees were in blossom everywhere.

Finally the boy burst forth: "Do you know what the message is I'm carrying from Pa to Christian Swain today?"

"No."

"Pa has at last given his consent for Barzillai and me to go with Reuben Swain to Wilmington the end of this month and work in his uncle Jethro's warehouses. I'm taking Pa's word to Christian Swain this morning about making the neccssary arrangements with Jethro Swain. Barzillai and I will leave with Reuben at the month's end. Isn't that marvelous news, Martitia?"

Martitia turned her head away. "Yes, Clarkson."

The boy went on: "Barzillai and I will become wealthy merchants someday and set up our own warehouses full of salt kegs and turpentine barrels. In a year I'll come riding back on my horse and tell you how I'm fast becoming a rich man. You'll think better of me when I wear fine store clothes from Wilmington."

The girl kept her head away.

Clarkson spoke gayly: "I will write you letters and tell you the fine things that I see in Wilmington: all about the schooners from the Indies and the sailors in the river harbor. You will like that, won't you?"

"Yes, Clarkson."

In September you went away and left me, Jonathan. Now Clarkson is going to leave me too. Must I always be left behind when the people I love go away?

"I'll send you trinkets, Martitia, that the schooners from the Indies bring in. Will you like that?"

"Yes."

"And will you write me letters next year in return, to say how the maypops are ripening in May at Centre as they are now, or how the cornfields look in July, or how the poplar leaves turn gold in the autumn?"

"Yes, Clarkson."

In sudden excess of irrepressible high spirits Clarkson took Martitia's hand. "Come, let's go eat maypops from the vines by the Meeting House. Addison says they're ripe. He brought some home yesterday. We'll celebrate Barzillai's and my going away."

They took a short cut through the fields.

The boy grew soberer. "My only sorrow is that Jonathan won't be home before we leave. Reuben can't wait longer than the end of the month to go. Barzillai and I can't tarry to see Jonathan. 'Twill be a year or more till we see him." He sighed.

They came to the white Meeting House grounds.

The maypop vines were thick with their purple flowers and sweet, pulpy fruit. The two young people sat on the ground to eat. East of the church was the quiet plot that was the Friends' burial ground.

Clarkson grinned at the girl suddenly. "Want to go into the burial ground and see where I'll be buried someday?"

Martitia looked frightened. But she followed Clarkson into the plot. She looked about her in awe at the stones which told the stories of birth-dates and death-dates at Centre.

"Here's where the Gardners lie, Martitia." Clarkson pointed. "There's Ma's mother, Abigail Pinkham. And there's Grandfather Daniel's wife, Eunice Hussey. She died a long, long time ago. By her side is a place for Grandfather Daniel to lie in someday."

"Whose are the three very little graves, Clarkson?"

"They belong to my two little brothers and my little sister who died as children. It was for their sakes Pa became a doctor. One after another the babies born to Pa and Ma here in Guilford died. Pa vowed he couldn't bear to see his own children die. So he set off in his sulky to Philadelphia in Pennsylvania to get some medical training. Ma stayed on the farm alone with Miriam who was a baby and ran things till Pa came back in his sulky with a medical diploma and a pair of merino sheep. After that none of Pa's children ever died. So Pa felt satisfied."

Martitia looked misty-eyed. "Doctor David has a loving heart. A loving heart is a beautiful thing."

Clarkson suddenly burst into irrepressible mirth. "Look, Martitia. There's a maypop vine growing on Grandma Eunice Hussey's grave. It's got a maypop on it too. I've a mind to eat that maypop. It looks extra large and fine."

Martitia shuddered. "Oh, Clarkson!"

But Clarkson leaned over and ate the maypop fruit from Grandma Eunice Hussey's grave. He peered at Martitia wickedly as he finished the maypop. "I give you leave to come up here and eat maypops off *my* grave someday, Martitia."

Martitia only gasped. She turned and fled out of the burial plot.

They went to Christian Swain's house. Martitia waited in the house with Abigail Swain while Clarkson talked to Christian and Reuben in the tanyard. Then they hurried home. Eunice was already putting dinner on the table.

Next day was what Martitia called "Sunday" but what the rest of the Gardners called "First Day." Martitia went with the family to silent worship in the morning. But after three hours of almost complete stillness Martitia was glad to let her tongue wag by the time afternoon came.

She helped Grandfather Daniel out to a chair on the front porch. Grandfather Daniel, with his clumsy attempt to be gay with Martitia, said he "had a mind to sit with his second mate and consider the number of barrels of whale oil the ship's crew had gathered during the last seven days."

The old man was obviously feeble. Martitia watched him with a catch of pain in her ribs. Would the old whaler who had been so kind to a frightened little second mate see another May weave its white web of dogwood blooms over Centre? Or would he hear no note of the blackbirds from his place up yonder by Eunice Hussey in the quiet grounds near the Meeting House?

Grandfather Daniel rested after his trip from kitchen

to porch. The three Gardner boys passed along the front in the direction of the cherry trees. They walked in a close group. It always touched Martitia to see their comradeship.

Grandfather Daniel watched them too. He spoke detachedly: "The brotherhood of those boys has always been a rare sight. One of them would die for any other of them. They are good boys, those grandsons of mine: these three and the two that are gone."

Martitia said nothing, only waited.

Grandfather Daniel went on. His far-away old voice sounded to the girl rather like the reading of the Book of Numbers in the Bible. "My grandson Barzillai is the most religious one of the boys. My grandson Addison is the most impulsive and the most easily discouraged. My grandson Clarkson is the most tender-hearted. My grandson Milton is a part-embodiment of the virtues of all the rest. But my grandson Jonathan was cast in the strongest mold of them all. He forms his own opinions and lives up to them. He will have enemies, as all strong men do. But no one will ever be able truly to say aught to my grandson Jonathan's uncredit. Jonathan's life will be full of success and honor."

Grandfather Daniel paused. Then he continued sternly: "We Gardners have always been full of industry and devotion to principle and the fear of God. We have prospered, and we have won the respect of others. We can die in peace."

As though too weary to continue, his voice stopped. Martitia sat so still that a bird hopped up the stone steps and peered at her fearlessly from close at hand.

Then Grandfather Daniel spoke in a stronger tone:

"Does thee know child, that my grandson Clarkson has set his heart upon thee? And has thee decided what to do about him?"

Martitia looked embarrassed. She did not answer.

Grandfather Daniel patted her head. "Say naught if thee does not wish to, child. Thy heart is thine own to shut or to open. If things had been somewhat otherwise I should have wished that my grandson Jonathan had been free to fasten his affections on so gentle and pretty a child as thee."

Martitia looked up swiftly. "And are your grandson Jonathan's affections then already bespoken, sir?"

Grandfather Daniel answered slowly: "Since they were children I think my grandson Jonathan and his cousin Sarah Gardner Mendenhall over in Jamestown have admired each other. Likely Jonathan and Sarah will wed someday. At any rate I've never heard my grandson Jonathan speak of any other female with admiration as he often speaks of Sarah Mendenhall. Sarah has a fine intellect like my grandson Jonathan's. Sarah can read Latin books as my grandson Jonathan can. The girl is full of thrift and industry also. She is renowned at Jamestown for her weaving and for her half-moon apple pies. Sarah is a trifle plainer than I fancy myself. But likely she makes up for that in her intrinsic virtues with Jonathan."

Martitia got up hurriedly, frightening the bird on the steps so that he flew away to the treetops. "I must go help Aunt Eunice. I see Ruth coming to you, sir."

She was gone before Grandfather Daniel could speak another word in praise of Sarah Gardner Mendenhall, the paragon of Jamestown! She ran upstairs and hid till suppertime.

At supper Eunice spoke suddenly to Grandfather Daniel: "Father, thee is not eating thy supper. Thee seemed always to enjoy thy victuals before. Is aught wrong with the food this evening?"

"No, Daughter. The wrong must be with my innards, not thy victuals. I feel strangely light-headed. I have a mind to go to my bed now without waiting for night."

Dr. David looked swiftly, intently, at his father. He rose quickly. "I'll 'company thee into thy room, Father."

Martitia watched Dr. David's face. She felt sudden fear. Never before had she heard Dr. David use the plain language of his Quaker faith to his father. She felt instinctively that something was dreadfully wrong.

Dr. David bent his deepest, gentlest look on his father. He half supported, half carried the shrunken old form out of the room. As he left he nodded to Eunice.

A hush fell over the rest of the Gardners. No one spoke for a minute. Then Eunice rose. She addressed Ruth.

"So be the will of the Lord. I think thy grandfather's time has come. Thy father has known for a long spell that this was coming. Thy father, as a physician, knows how these things must be. Come with me, Daughter. Go with me to thy grandfather. Next to his own son David, thy grandfather has loved thee best."

Eunice and Ruth left the room. Martitia and the boys waited in silent awe. After a while Eunice came back. She spoke to Martitia.

"David's father is dying. Do thee redd up the kitchen alone. Later on thee must come with the boys to the old man's room. He would wish it so. He has often said that thee was like another granddaughter to him."

Martitia made the kitchen immaculate. The boys talked in hushed tones. Much later on Eunice came to the door and beckoned to them.

They went into Grandfather Daniel's room.

Ruth was kneeling by the old man's side. She held one of his shrunken hands, wetting it with her painful, unaccustomed tears.

Dr. David sat on the bed by his father. Martitia heard his voice repeating the Psalms. He never wavered in his deep murmur of grand old words:

"The Lord is my Shepherd; I shall not want. He maketh me to lie down in green pastures; He leadeth me beside the still waters. He restoreth my soul . . ." On and on went the beautiful, deathless words: "Thy rod and thy staff, they comfort me. Thou preparest a table before me in the presence of mine enemies: Thou anointest my head with oil . . ."

Presently Martitia, from her chair by the wall, knew that Grandfather Daniel could hear the words no more.

But it was not till dawn came and the sun over the poplar trees sent a long finger of pure light through the round porthole to fall on Grandfather Daniel's seaworthy face that the heart of the old whaler stopped beating at last.

Martitia got up stiffly from her chair and went with the others out of the still room and left Dr. David and Ruth there. The boys filed out to the barn in silence. Eunice and Martitia turned toward the kitchen.

As though sensing what filled the girl's heart so full she was utterly incapable of speech, Eunice led Martitia out on the back porch to the morning-glories and the sunshine and the sounds of stirring farm life.

"Look at the sunlight, child. Be thankful that it is given thee to live in the sunshine for a while and then to go through the sunshine to a better world than this. I know well how the passing of my husband's father has reminded thee of thy own father's and mother's passing. But remember this: The passing of old people or of people of any age is not rightly a matter for sadness, but a matter for triumph. 'Tis we in our human weakness who manufacture the sadness, not they. They are happier than ever they were before. Look up, Martitia, and be glad."

Martitia lifted her face to the sunshine.

CHAPTER XIII

A Visitor Arrives

"COME QUICKLY, MARTITIA. There is a gentleman who has arrived in a gig at the door. He
says he wishes to see you. He will not tell his name to
me. He only asked me in a cool voice if this were the
Gardner house and bade me go fetch 'Miss Martitia
Howland.' It's a very elegant gentleman with a broad-
cloth suit and a gold-headed cane and a beaver hat. It's
likely someone your uncle James has sent at last to fetch
you to Richmond."

Ruth spoke breathlessly to Martitia, who was in the
back yard of the Gardner place. Martitia, returning from
feeding the turkeys, still held a bucket with a few grains
of corn sticking to its insides. Martitia turned pale.

"Perhaps there's some mistake. Perhaps it's a gentleman who wishes to see Doctor David as a physician. Or
maybe 'tis one of Aunt Eunice's relatives from Randolph
County."

"Since when did I not know Ma's relatives from Randolph County? And since when could I not recognize a sick patient when I saw one at the door? No, the gentleman quite plainly asked for you."

Martitia smoothed her blue homespun skirts nervously. "Where are Aunt Eunice and Doctor David?"

"Pa went to the barn to physic an ailing calf. Ma went with him. I was all alone at the house when the gentleman came. The boys haven't come in from the fields yet. It's a long while till dinnertime."

"Where did you leave the gentleman?" Martitia's voice was a wisp of terrified thistledown on the May air.

"I left him sitting on the front porch. He was tapping his gold-headed cane in great impatience. Do you hurry up, Martitia, and go through the house to the porch to see him. If you want, I'll go fetch Pa from the barn."

"Yes, I want Doctor David."

"Go ahead, then. I'll go for Pa this instant."

Martitia hesitated at the foot of the back porch. Then she resolutely mounted the steps, passed through the kitchen, and marched out on the front porch, still carrying her tin bucket.

She took one look at the gentleman with the gold-headed cane. Then she turned pale as unbaked light bread.

"Uncle James!"

The gentleman on the porch rose. He came forward and kissed Martitia lightly. The gold-headed cane he kept tucked under one arm.

"Well, child! I'm glad to see you. Your aunt Margaret has worried over you badly. I told her you were all right. But you do look pale. Have these abominable Quakers not given you proper food? I shall set that to rights promptly. You're going back with me tonight to Richmond. Not another night are you to spend under the roof of common Quakers like this greedy fellow David Gardner."

For a moment Martitia stood speechless. Then she found words in a rush. "Surely," thought Martitia, "the winter at Centre has taught me courage I never knew before." She was amazed at the intrepid sound of her own voice when she answered Uncle James.

"You have no right, Uncle James, to speak untruths of Doctor David. He is the finest gentleman that ever lived. To be a Quaker is not a sin. It is something to be proud of. I stayed here with Doctor David and his family because I wished to stay, not because they kept me. They have kind hearts, and they love me. When no one else cared about me, they took me in and welcomed me. It is only now, after nearly a year, that you have bothered to come from Richmond to fetch me back with you."

Uncle James interrupted dryly: "It was not merely to fetch you back with me that I made all the long trip from Virginia, Martitia. That would have been very foolish. My silver business required me to go to South Carolina. I contrived to return by way of Jamestown, North Carolina, in order to attend to this family matter. It would be ridiculous to suppose that I should leave my entire business affairs for reasons of mere sentiment, such as fetching home my wife's niece. You are full of romantic notions, like your mother."

Martitia answered firmly: "If I had been Grandfather Daniel's niece he would have come to fetch me, Uncle James. He told me so."

"And who is Grandfather Daniel, pray?"

Martitia spoke in a low voice: "He was Doctor David's father. He died two weeks ago."

"Humph. And where is this country Quaker, this Doctor David Gardner, whom you admire so much that you are rude to your own kin to defend?"

Martitia heard footsteps behind her. A strong, courteous voice spoke: "Here is that country Quaker named David Gardner. You are welcome to my home. May I inquire your name and the business which brings us the honor of your visit?"

Uncle James extended his hand. "I am James Randolph, of Virginia, sir. This young lady here is my niece. My business is simple. I have come by gig from Jamestown to fetch my niece home with me to Richmond. I am obliged to you for your hospitality in her behalf."

Dr. David took the outstretched hand. "Hospitality to Martitia is like hospitality to one of my own children." He smiled at the girl.

The face of the man from Virginia stiffened. "Your hospitality is of a strange sort, sir. You have kept my niece under your roof against the expressed wishes of her family and against the laws of the state in which you live."

Dr. David looked down into Uncle James's cool eyes. "Permit me to point out to you that I have in no way violated the laws of North Carolina in keeping your niece here."

Uncle James showed some rearrangement of preconceived ideas in his face. He spoke more suavely: "What do you mean by that, sir?"

Dr. David answered deliberately: "To put the matter in simple language, I notified the courts of Guilford County last October of the presence of an orphan in my home. The proper authorities have been aware of Martitia's presence here. At the next Court Day in Guilford I shall enter a plea for the guardianship of Martitia. My son, who is legally trained, will return the first of June to my home. He will prepare the case for me. The course of legal action in Guilford County proceeds with no more haste than do certain uncles whom I know proceed with haste in coming to that county to claim their nieces."

Uncle James reddened. "The abominable conditions of your roads in Carolina are responsible for my long delay in coming to claim Martitia. No intelligent man would venture to take a trip by the stagecoaches in midwinter. It required the coming of spring to render the roads passable for a gentleman."

Dr. David smiled. "We are sorry that our rough Carolina roads and manners suffer in comparison with the roads and manners of Virginia. It is likely that you may feel also that our rough Carolina laws seem harsh to an outsider."

Uncle James frowned. "You provoke me intentionally, sir. By the advice of my lawyer I hoped to settle this matter of Martitia's guardianship outside the law courts. But since you ask for it, let me enlighten your ignorance on legal matters. You may enter plea for the child's guardianship but you will never be granted it. You are a Quaker. Martitia is of the Protestant Presbyterian faith. By the law of North Carolina no Quaker may become the guardian of a child of another religious sect."

Uncle James stroked his gold-headed cane. Martitia gasped. Dr. David looked unperturbed.

"Your Richmond lawyer seems only partially informed on North Carolina statutes. My son Jonathan is well versed in our state's laws. He has informed me of certain discriminations in guardianship against Quakers. But he has also informed me of what your own lawyer seems unaware. By the Act of 1762 of this state, a man of the Protestant faith may not *will* his child to a Quaker. But there is nothing in the North Carolina statutes which prevents the courts themselves from *appointing* a Quaker to the guardianship of a child of another religious sect. And Martitia's father left no will."

Uncle James looked disconcerted. "Are you certain of your facts, sir?"

"I am always certain of my facts when my son Jonathan advances them."

Uncle James ruminated a moment. "My main case need not depend on your Quakery. My lawyer tells me that the common law of North Carolina will undoubtedly award the child to me as next of male kin. The courts of the state will naturally make me guardian of my own niece in preference to you who are no kin of hers at all."

Dr. David looked steadily down into Uncle James's eyes. "That may be, or it may not be. When my son Jonathan comes home he will prepare a case for me."

Uncle James stroked his gold-headed cane again. He spoke with emphasis: "I will go to the county seat of Guilford immediately and enter my plea for guardianship of my niece."

Dr. David smiled. "The quarterly courts of Guilford are held at the county seat on the third Mondays of February, May, August, and November. The court day for May in Guilford is already over. You may enter your plea on the docket, but you will have to wait for your decision till court convenes again on the third Monday of August. You will have a long wait in Greensborough."

Uncle James abruptly stopped fingering his cane. He frowned again. "Then I will return in my hired gig to Jamestown over your abominable roads. I will go from there over your abominable roads to the county seat and enter my plea on the docket. After that I will return to civilization in Richmond. I will put the entire matter into my lawyer's hands. We will return to Guilford in August and meet you in court. Then justice will have its proper course. Martitia will become my ward."

"As you like." Dr. David bowed.

"When the case comes up for hearing in August you may be sure that the courts will take into consideration the financial status of the orphan's uncle as opposed to that of a mere country Quaker of no means."

Dr. David looked firm. "I think you misjudge the nature of our Guilford County judiciary. Money will not buy our courts."

"We shall see what we shall see."

"That is true. We shall indeed see what we shall see."

Uncle James turned to Martitia. His face looked troubled. "I don't want to make you a pawn in a court struggle, child. There's nothing for me to gain in assuming your guardianship. I'm a rich man. Your father's property is infinitesimal. But your aunt Margaret and I feel that we have a duty toward Peyton blood. This fellow, David Gardner, wishes to secure control of your father's little estate. He is no kin of yours. Come with me today and let my lawyer handle this business for us. Your aunt and your cousins expect you in Richmond."

Martitia paled. She looked toward Dr. David. He

made no gesture toward her. She straightened her shoulders as a soldier would. She answered Uncle James in a firm voice:

"I'm sorry to seem ungrateful, sir. I'm truly grateful to you and Aunt Margaret. But I love the Gardners. I'm going to stay here always if the courts will let me."

Uncle James bowed briefly. He descended the steps. He climbed in his gig and set off toward Jamestown. Dr. David reached out his hand and drew Martitia gently toward his side. Together they watched the gig disappear.

"Your uncle James is trying hard to do his duty. But he's also trying hard to outwit a country Quaker named David Gardner. He'll never do it. Not while I've got a son named Jonathan!"

Eunice appeared from within the house. She came up with her soundless step. "Did thee send the Randolph fellow packing, David?"

"I sent the Randolph fellow packing." Dr. David's voice held well-controlled but unmistakable anger.

Eunice surveyed him a moment. Then she said quietly: "Thee is thinking 'dammit,' David. I am ashamed of thee. Thee ought not to swear, being a Friend."

Dr. David broke into an enormous laugh. "Woman, you are too keen-eyed. You must not read a man's mind like that. Go back to your pots and pans. I begin to grow hungry for my midday meal."

Eunice went back into the house. Dr. David looked at Martitia. "Come what may in life, 'tis better to laugh than to cry. Keep your chin up. When Jonathan comes home next month he'll know how to prepare a case that will send your uncle James packing for keeps in August. Jonathan is a better lawyer from his law books alone, before ever he studies with Judge Debow, than your uncle James's city lawyer is in Richmond."

Martitia relaxed. Nothing too dreadful could happen if Dr. David was laughing again! The horn sounded. Dinner was ready. The boys would be back soon. Dr. David followed Eunice inside. Martitia ran upstairs to brush her hair.

Suddenly she saw that she was still carrying the tin bucket with the remains of the turkeys' breakfast in it. She sat down by the window and began to laugh. How must she have looked to elegant Uncle James, appearing with a tin bucket of turkey food in her small Peyton fingers! Martitia laughed until she cried. Then she stopped. A startled look was on her face.

Why, I was laughing like a Gardner!

Very meditatively she descended the steps. The boys had come in. The family was seated at table. Dr. David was just finishing the tale of the morning's happenings. Martitia heard him say as she entered:

"So Mr. James Randolph went away in his hired gig along the road toward Jamestown."

Martitia saw Clarkson rise from the table. The boy stalked silently toward the door on to the front porch. His handsome face was dark.

"Where are you going, Son?" called Dr. David.

"I'm going after Uncle James and knock him out of his hired gig till he bites the dust, if it's the last thing I ever do," said Clarkson.

Dr. David roared with delight. "Can't say but what I'd like to see Uncle James's face a bit dusty myself, Son. But he's too far on his way for you to come up to him now. Uncle James was going at top speed when last I set eyes on him. He's got a half-hour's start on you. Best to let Jonathan set Uncle James mental teeth in the dust in August. Come back here and eat your dinner."

Clarkson came glowering back. Martitia looked at him with admiration.

CHAPTER XIV

Two Travelers Set Forth

MARTITIA SAT ON A STOOL in the middle of the kitchen, with a round bowl inverted on the top of her head. From below the bowl her small face peered out comically. Her eyes looked worried.

"Are you *sure* you know how to cut my hair just exactly as Doctor David cuts it, Addison?"

"Perfectly sure, or I wouldn't have offered to do it. I've seen Pa cut it twice now: once in November and once in February. I can cut it exactly the same way. The bowl will keep it from flying about."

"I think I ought to wait till Doctor David comes home from the tanyard."

"No, Martitia. Pa may not be home till noon. It should take Christian Swain that long to finish mending Clarkson's saddle. Pa and Clarkson won't be in much before dinnertime."

"Where's Barzillai? You said he was going to help with the cutting of my hair. I don't like your doing it all by yourself. You mightn't get it straight."

"Barzillai's finishing up at the barn. He'll be in soon. Pa said none of us boys need work today except for tending the stock. Since it's the last day Barzillai and Clarkson will be here before they leave for Wilmington, Pa's giving us a day off from the fields. Here's Barzillai now."

Barzillai, big and slow-moving, loomed in the door from the back porch. He surveyed Martitia with the bowl on her head. He spoke amusedly: "Are you ready for the shearing, Martitia?"

"I'm no sheep, Barzillai. Stop talking like that."

Barzillai winked at Addison. Addison wiggled his ears. Martitia moved uneasily on the tall stool. "I think I'll change my mind and not have my hair cut now. Take the bowl off my head, Addison, and let me down."

Addison tied the sheet tighter about Martitia's neck. He appeared not to hear her protesting voice. "Come on, Barzillai. You take a pair of shears too. We'll each cut half of Martitia's hair. We'll sort of meet in the middle at the back. Are you ready?"

"Ready," said Barzillai.

Before Martitia could change her mind and get loose from the prisoning sheet on her tall perch she heard the shears begin to go "snip, snip" on either side of her small ears. "Now do be careful," she wailed. "I just want it to come halfway to my shoulders."

"Snip, snip," went the two pairs of shears. Two masculine heads bent over the bowl intently.

Presently Martitia heard an exclamation of dismay:

"Somebody's got off on the wrong track somewhere," murmured Addison in an agonized voice. "Your hair is an inch shorter on one side than on the other, Martitia. It doesn't meet in the back. Maybe we'll have to scallop it."

"Oh, Addison, Addison! Don't *scallop* my hair. Let me down!"

"How would it be, Barzillai, to sort of make Martitia's hair in little half-moons at the bottom, like Ma's apple pies?"

"That's a good idea, Addison. Half-moons are really scallops."

Martitia began to wail and flap about on the stool. "Let me down! Let me down! I won't *have* my hair all scalloped into half-moons!"

"Snip, snip," went the shears. Martitia wailed more loudly. A voice suddenly spoke from the front door:

"What are you boys up to now?"

Addison and Barzillai jumped. Martitia looked in utter relief toward the front door. There stood Dr. David. His shining eyes surveyed Martitia and the bowl and Addison and Barzillai.

"Want a helping hand with the shearing of that lamb, boys? If Clarkson hadn't taken the horses to the barn he'd doubtless have a word to say to you about this."

"Well, sir," answered Addison uneasily, "the lamb sort of jiggled about on the shearing table. It's fleece got a little snipped in places."

Dr. David came over to Martitia and lifted the bowl off her perspiring forehead. "Give me the shears, boys. I'll finish the job." He suppressed a laugh.

Addison and Barzillai hastily handed over their shears. They retired precipitately toward the back porch. Martitia could hear their gales of unholy merriment through the window as they disappeared in the direction of the barn.

Doctor David examined Martitia's uneven locks quizzically. "A man who's barbered twelve children ought to know how to cut the hair of a shorn Samson, let alone a Delilah. We'll set this straight in a jiffy."

He expertly clipped and snipped. Martitia sat still on her stool, looking reassured.

"Never saw a finer job," announced Dr. David finally. He untied the sheet and blew off the hairs from Martitia's slim neck. "If your aunt Eunice tolerated a mirror about the place you could see what a pretty little Delilah you look now."

Martitia thanked him. She ran upstairs to her own room. She shut her door carefully. If Ruth or Aunt Eunice were to come up from the springhouse now Martitia did not mean to be caught indulging in un-Quakerly doings. With one ear cocked toward the closed door, she opened her tin trunk. From the very bottom she took out three things. The first was a little square of looking-glass. The second was an oval miniature with a gold rim. The third was an old but beautifully laundered white muslin dress.

She examined her hair in the looking-glass. Dr. David was right! She smiled with relief. No half-moons appeared there! Exactly at the right length, halfway to her small shoulders, hung the dark, fine cloud. She tied her accustomed narrow blue ribbon about it. She put on the muslin dress. She added the gold-rimmed miniature pin in front. Then she inspected herself once more in the mirror. Very like the miniature itself she looked, decided Martitia.

Heavy-lidded blue eyes looked dreamily back at her. A slim, pointed face showed softly drooping lips. The firm little chin belied the sensitive mouth above. Dark hair formed a frame.

So immersed in the vanities of this world did Martitia become, patting her gathered skirts, smoothing her hair, retying her ribbon, that the sound of the dinner horn below startled her from a revery.

She finished primping and went downstairs. Her first glance went straight to Clarkson at the dinner table. The black-eyed boy stared back at her. He smiled his matchless smile. Martitia looked satisfied. She sat down by Dr. David.

After dinner Clarkson wheedled his mother: "Ma, can you spare Martitia? I want her to go with me to salt the sheep for the last time. You can't refuse me anything on my last day at Centre. It'll be twelve months or longer before I ride home again to visit."

Eunice said: "Go with the boy, Martitia, since his heart is set upon having thee."

Martitia and Clarkson set out for the wood's plot. Sandy went with them. Clarkson carried the salt sack over one shoulder. As soon as they were out of hearing of the house the boy spoke softly: "You look pretty today, Martitia. Not that you don't always look pretty. But maybe it's the white dress or the fancy pin that makes you look so uncommonly elegant. I never saw the pin before. Isn't the face on it yours?"

"Yes, my mother painted me so at twelve. She had a real gift for painting."

"Do you ever miss your own picture-making, Martitia, since you came here? Ruth says you used to paint pictures at your father's house. You never make them any more, do you?"

"No, I've nothing to make pictures with now. But it doesn't matter. I never truly had a gift like my mother. I think I was always fitted to be a housewife instead. I love the weaving and the butter-making and the cooking. Maybe the painting made my hands defter at the loom. But truly I love the weaving, Clarkson."

The boy stared at her, color mantling his face. "And do you love the Gardners as well as the Gardner weaving, Martitia?"

"I love the Gardners."

"*All* of them?"

Martitia nodded.

"*Some* more than others?"

Martitia grew pink. She stared at the ground.

"Next year when I come riding back I'll be a man, Martitia. I'll be twenty. You'll have to answer me then. If your uncle James has taken you to Richmond I'll come all the way there to find you."

Martitia kept silent, her face turned pinkly toward the ground.

Stillness enveloped the boy and girl. They arrived at the wood's plot. Clarkson filled the salting log. As he emptied the salt sack he seemed also to unload his mood of gravity and poignancy. He began to sing on the way back home along the wooded path:

> *"There's a lady goes*
> *In stocking toes.*
> *She's got blue eyes*
> *And a button nose.*
> *But* when *she will laugh*
> *Nobody knows."*

Martitia looked at him. She smiled.

Clarkson grinned back. "Will you learn to laugh before I come home next year?"

"I'm learning now. Jonathan bade me learn to laugh too.'"

"It was always Jonathan you obeyed from the start, never me." The boy sighed.

" 'Twas always Jonathan I felt fear for, never you."

The boy's face lighted. He began to roar again:

> *"There's a lady goes*
> *In stocking toes.*
> *She's got blue eyes*
> *And a button nose . . ."*

He stopped suddenly in the middle of the path. "Your painted brooch is loose, Martitia. Let me fasten it for you."

"All right, Clarkson. Fasten it."

They paused a second. With the painted brooch attended to, the two young people walked on together slowly through the afternoon of late May. Sandy ran ahead of them.

Next morning Martitia stood on the front porch with Clarkson. It was only shortly after sunup. The rest of the family was inside. Barzillai's and Clarkson's horses champed at the hitching post, waiting for the beginning of the long trip down to Wilmington and Jethro Swain's warehouses. They would go by Jamestown and stop long enough to see Milton. Barzillai's setter dog raced and barked about, apparently eager to be off.

Clarkson turned to the girl. His laughing eyes were grave. "Come with me to the cherry tree, Martitia."

The girl went with him, her slim face drooping. Under the cherry tree lay a familiar brown form. It was Sandy. The black-haired boy dropped on his knees by the collie.

"Good boy, Sandy. You stayed here all during breakfast, like I told you to, didn't you? Listen to me now, Sandy. Give me your paw."

Sandy's unwavering eyes looked into Clarkson's face. The dog studied his master's face intently. He held out his paw. Martitia stood watching the two, the boy and the dog. For a moment Clarkson seemed to forget her. He talked softly to the dog.

"Next to the family, you're the best thing I own, Sandy. But I'm not taking you with me today, as the other boys take their dogs. I'm going to leave you with Martitia. You must take good care of her for me, Sandy. Except when Pa sends you to round up the sheep you must stay with Martitia and see that nothing ever frightens or hurts her. Can you remember that, boy? Will you take care of your new mistress as carefully as I would try to take care of her if I were here? Keep her safe till I come back, Sandy."

As though he could almost understand the words, Sandy stared at his master. He whined in a low, disturbed manner. He nuzzled his pointed nose against Clarkson's black head. He gave several sharp, anxious barks, as though to say: "Take me with you, *please*."

Clarkson stroked the heavy coat. He reached up gently and drew Martitia down to her knees beside him.

"Give your paw to your new mistress, Sandy."

Sandy whined pitifully. Almost in a human way he looked from Clarkson to Martitia. Clarkson took the dog's paw and put it carefully into Martitia's hand.

"Take care of her, Sandy, till I come back."

Sandy whined.

Clarkson squeezed Martitia's tiny fingers. He rose, leaving the girl kneeling by the big dog.

"Stay with her, Sandy. I'm going now. Don't come."

Martitia blinked back the tears. She stared after the boy till he disappeared up the hill out of her sight.

CHAPTER XV

The Gardner Lawyer

JUNE THE FOURTH dawned in enchanted light and stillness. Martitia did not wait for true daylight to come before she got up and dressed. Today was the day that Jonathan would come home! Today was her seventeenth birthday. It took Martitia an unwonted time to adjust her starched blue homespun dress and to brush her dark hair. She descended the steps before anyone else in the house was stirring. Not even Eunice had yet appeared.

Martitia went out on the back porch and got the pitcher for the water. She skirted the house to the well, loving the feel of the soft morning mist and coolness on her cheeks. Out of the mist from somewhere came Sandy to meet her. She leaned over and patted him. At the well she let the rope down, peering over the side to see the brass-rimmed wooden bucket hit the water deep below. The bucket came back up brimming with cold well water. She filled her pitcher and went slowly back to the house. Inside she heard Eunice rattling the pans for breakfast.

159

Martitia drew a deep breath and smiled. It was on such a morning not yet a year ago that Jonathan had stood on his head on this very back porch. It was on such a morning that Jonathan had wetted her black shoes and stockings with the over-brimming basin of well water. Today he was coming home again! By sunset Jonathan's bay mare would appear up the dusty road from the direction of Hillsborough. From today forward, till autumn came, a pair of keen hazel eyes would peer down at Martitia in veiled amusement. A tall, spare young man would tease Martitia unmercifully.

Martitia went inside and began to help Eunice and Ruth with breakfast. Dr. David came rollicking into the kitchen. His face showed a radiance it had lacked for the whole six days since Barzillai and Clarkson had ridden away to Wilmington. He spoke to Eunice gayly.

"Woman, hurry with breakfast. Is not our eldest-born son coming home today? Will not our lawyer-son be back by sundown? I've a mind to turn a somersault like Addison."

"Tut, tut, David. Thee must remember thee is a middleaged man, the father of twelve sons and daughters. They come and they go, these children of ours. Thee is no young whippersnapper to get so excited over one son's return."

She shook her head in reproof. But Martitia noted that her eyes were bright.

Addison looked as gay as his father at breakfast. The youngest Gardner son had gone about forlornly for six days, openly missing his brothers. Now he could scarcely contain himself for joy over Jonathan's return. Milton, who came home often, was busy with final study at Dr. Lindsay's. He could not be here for Jonathan's return. Addison was lonely.

"Why are you so solemn, Martitia? Aren't you glad Jonathan's coming today? I believe you're afraid of Jonathan."

Martitia lifted her head. Her eyes were veiled with their lashes. "I'm not solemn. Only thinking. Yes, I'm glad Jonathan's coming. And yes, I'm afraid of Jonathan."

Addison laughed in delight. "I thought so. Well, you can tell Sandy to protect you from Jonathan. Sandy won't let anyone get near you since Clarkson left."

After breakfast Martitia set out for the springhouse. Sandy went with her. Not a move of the girl's went unnoticed now by the brown collie. Before going to her weaving Martitia confused Sandy by continuing on down the slope to the apple orchard below. She selected a soft, rather overripe red apple from a tree there. She put the apple in her pocket. Then she returned demurely to her weaving.

Around sundown the whole Gardner family waited on the front porch for Jonathan's bay mare and her rider to appear up the road. Only Martitia slipped away and left the house by the back. Sandy saw and followed her. Martitia skirted the house secretively and approached the side gate where the road entered the yard. She climbed up into the mulberry tree from whose wide branches the Gardner boys had first descended upon her in Dr. David's gig last summer. Her blue dress disappeared into the thick leaves. She sat very still. Sandy lay below.

After a while a bay mare with a rider on her back appeared in the road that ascended the slope to the house among the pines and poplars. A dog followed at the horse's heels.

Martitia's eyes began to shine. She reached into the pocket of her skirt with one small hand. She brought out a soft, rather overripe red apple. As the horse with the rider got close to the gate, preparing to turn in, Martitia drew back her arm and hurled the apple squarely at the approaching rider.

"Plop!" went the apple against the rider's sleeve. "Splash!" went the soft pulp in all directions.

The girl drew back into the leaves and laughed silently.

Without hesitation the rider hurled himself off his mare's back and made a running leap for the tree where Martitia crouched. He climbed upward. Jonathan's brown head and hazel eyes appeared in the leaves at Martitia's side.

Jonathan stared at her unbelievingly. "Martitia, was it *you* that threw that apple? I thought it was Addison or Pa. Surely it wasn't *you!*"

Martitia stopped laughing. She looked frightened. But she answered bravely: "Didn't *you* throw apples at *me* when I came to live at Centre? It's only fair I should throw apples back."

Jonathan stared at her for a minute. Then he put his head back and broke into a howl of delight. "Why, Martitia, you're defying me! You actually are *defying* me. And you're learning to laugh!"

Martitia grinned sheepishly. She dropped down into the lower branches and made for the ground below. Jonathan followed her.

Addison came running from the porch. Then Ruth came after. Dr. David left the porch and strode over the grass to greet his eldest son. Only Eunice waited on the steps.

Her hands outspread themselves as her son came up the yard. "Thee is welcome home, Jonathan. Our lawyer-son is welcome home." She kissed him on the face, reaching her short height up on tiptoe to attain his hard, healthy cheek. Martitia watched them.

Supper that evening was a satisfying meal. In spite of Grandfather Daniel's empty chair, in spite of the absence of Clarkson and Barzillai and Milton, Martitia saw contentment on the faces of the Gardners tonight. Jonathan was home again!

In the candlelight his magnificent forehead showed its fine, strong sweep. His hazel eyes glowed intelligently. He told in a deep voice of Hillsborough and the life at Mr. Bingham's school. He spoke more than usual. Martitia listened with her head bent forward.

Jonathan turned finally to the girl. His stern mouth softened. "Pa tells me that your uncle James Randolph is causing you and him a peck of worry, Martitia. Don't lose heart. Judge Debow was in Hillsborough the day before I left. He loaned me his new Haywood, just over from Raleigh. With that new Haywood we'll draw up a case that will send your uncle James packing in August."

"What is Haywood, Jonathan?"

Jonathan answered solemnly: "Haywood is a sort of tree that grows over around Raleigh. It produces a crop of hay, Martitia."

Martitia turned a painful red. Jonathan grinned diabolically.

Dr. David intervened: "Haywood is a law book, Martitia. Tomorrow morning we'll go over the matter of your uncle James in full: you and Jonathan and I. You can come to my office after breakfast, before Jonathan leaves for the fields."

"Going to set me to work in the fields immediately, are you, sir?" Jonathan looked with mock pathos toward his father.

"Yes, Son. With Barzillai and Clarkson gone, I've got to find two fellows to hire. Don't know how I'll manage to pay them. But the farm needs five men working all the time in summer. Milton won't be home till July. His medical course doesn't end till then. I need you."

"If you owned black slaves like other well-to-do North Carolina men you'd have no trouble, Pa," exploded Addison.

"You know no true Friend will hold a fellow-creature in bondage, Son."

"Cousin George Mendenhall over at Jamestown is a good Friend, and he owns a hundred slaves."

"Cousin George Mendenhall only buys his slaves in order to train them for trades and send them as freed men to Indiana and Iowa. You know that, Addison." Jonathan spoke quietly.

Martitia asked in a quick voice: "Is your cousin George Mendenhall in Jamestown the father of Sarah Gardner Mendenhall, Jonathan?"

Jonathan looked startled. "Where did you ever hear of Sarah Gardner Mendenhall, Martitia?"

Martitia hesitated. "Somebody in the family mentioned how good a Latin scholar was Sarah and how fine were her half-moon apple pies and her weaving."

Jonathan spoke with enthusiasm: "Yes, Sarah is a remarkable female. But she is not George Mendenhall's daughter. She is the daughter of Abel Mendenhall."

He turned to his father. "Pa, why don't we take Martitia over to Jamestown in July when Milton aims to finish his examinations? We could visit at Cousin Abel's home. Ma hasn't had a trip from home since she went to New Garden to Yearly Meeting two years ago. 'Twould do her and Martitia good to eat food of other folks' cooking. Ruth too. Milton could 'company us home."

"That's a first-rate idea, Son. We'll do it."

Eunice seemed pleased. Martitia sat pondering the matter.

Ruth spoke up: "I'll stay with the Macys. I've no use for idle trips. But Martitia could likely get Sarah Mendenhall to teach her some new weaves at the loom. Sarah is smart as a whip."

Martitia threw back her chin. "I don't need any remarkable female in Jamestown to teach me new weaves. I can learn everything I want by myself."

She flounced out of the room. Her last glance in Jonathan's direction showed that young man with a look of sheer amazement on his face.

Next morning after breakfast Martitia went with Dr. David and Jonathan over to Dr. David's office. They settled down. Jonathan took a book from under his arm.

"Pa, I burned down a whole candle of Ma's last night studying this new edition of Mr. John Haywood's book."

He held up a dark, thick volume of moderate dimensions. He opened the cover and indicated the flyleaf. Martitia stared at the inscription:

REPORTS OF CASES
adjudged in the
Superior Courts of Law and Equity
of the
STATE OF NORTH CAROLINA
By John Haywood, Esq.
Second Edition
Raleigh
1832

"Pa, on page 350 of this book is the answer to our problem about the guardianship of Martitia. I've found the solution. There's a ruling here of the Superior Court of North Carolina on a guardianship case similar to Martitia's. From that ruling I can work up a case which will defeat Mr. James Randolph at every turn in August." He extended the book to his father. "Here, Pa, you take the book and read the case on page 350. It's Mills versus McAllister. I'll explain the matter to Martitia in plainer terms, without legal words."

Dr. David took the book and went over to stand by the clear light at the window.

Jonathan faced Martitia. "Here's the case. There was a child here in North Carolina who was left an orphan. Two men entered pleas for her guardianship. One was her uncle. One was a neighbor who was no kin. The uncle lived in another state, some four or five hundred miles away."

"That's like Uncle James," said Martitia.

"It certainly is," answered Jonathan. "That's just the point. Well, the neighbor lived quite near to the orphaned child and near to the child's property."

"That's like Doctor David."

"It is indeed," agreed Jonathan triumphantly. "When the case was appealed to the Superior Court of North Carolina for a final decision, the Supreme Court decided that the neighbor and not the uncle should be appointed guardian to the orphan. The argument was that the uncle, being four or five hundred miles away, could not be supervised by the North Carolina Courts as to his treatment of the orphan or his handling of the orphan's property. On the other hand, the neighbor who lived close by, here in North Carolina itself, could be closely supervised by the court as to treatment of the orphan and handling of the orphan's property."

"Didn't the fact that the uncle was kin to the orphan child, and the neighbor was not kin, have any influence on the decision, Jonathan?

Jonathan stared at Martitia. "You know, you have a right clear brain, Martitia. I wouldn't have thought to hear you ask a good legal question like that. Well, the odd part of the matter was that the uncle's kinship in this case was held against him, not for him, by the courts. The uncle's kinship made him subject to inherit the orphan's property in the event of the orphan's death. The courts opined that the uncle mightn't be too careful of the health and long life of the orphan if he was set to inherit the orphan's estate upon death. Whereas the neighbor, who was no kin, held no chance of inheritance; therefore the neighbor was thought likelier to cherish the orphan's health and long life."

"And so the neighbor was appointed the guardian, Jonathan?

"Yes, Martitia. Just as Pa will be appointed your guardian in August when I finish making out a case for this affair. What the Supreme Court of a state rules once is well-nigh law after that."

Martitia could only nod in mute excitement.

Dr. David came over from the window. He looked at Jonathan with pride. "You've hit the nail on the head with this case, Son. When Uncle James Randolph comes riding back to North Carolina in August he'll find what another uncle found when he came riding from a far state to claim an orphan niece in North Carolina."

Martitia fled without speaking lest Jonathan see the tears she could no longer hide. That laughter of his which lurked always so close behind the hazel eyes might descend upon her and engulf her. Her face, though, gleamed through its tears. She would be a Gardner daughter in August!

CHAPTER XVI

Under the Mulberry Trees

"WHAT ARE YOU mumbling about, all to your-self, Martitia?"

Martitia turned beet-red. She faced Jonathan from her seat on the lowest of the back-porch steps.

"I'm practicing spelling words correctly. Please don't listen to me, Jonathan."

Jonathan arranged his long self beside the girl. "You're always trying to change yourself, aren't you? Since I went away last September you've changed yourself a great deal. I hardly recognize you as the same girl."

Martitia's lips drooped. "You don't like the way I've changed myself?"

"Yes, I like it very much. You're not afraid of every-thing as you were last year. How did you do it?"

"By watching the Gardners. No Gardner ever seems to be afraid of anything. Even the Gardners' dog faced a wolf unafraid. I determined to pattern myself after the Gardners."

"You're not even afraid of *me* any more?"

Martitia surveyed him from beneath drooped eye-lashes. "Only a very little bit."

Jonathan roared. Then he sobered. "You've learned to work too. I've watched you all these five days since I came home from Hillsborough. Every day you've gone down to the springhouse and worked for hours at your weaving. Ma says you've grown into a beautiful weaver. Ma depends on you like she did on Louisa."

Martitia flushed. "I have to confess that I'm still lazy. I hate to get up mornings and go down to the loom. I have to struggle with my laziness all the time. I reckon you couldn't understand a person's having to strive so to overcome a fault."

The young man surveyed her with a level glance. "I can understand that. I've got a dire fault of my own I've struggled with ever since I can remember. It's one that is like to stand between me and my life's best ambition too."

The girl lifted her eyes to him. "What is it, Jonathan? Tell me."

"I've never talked of it to anyone. But it'll be apparent enough when I start my law practice. I have a painful diffidence at speaking in public. I have no oratorical flourish. When I shall have to plead cases at the bar I'll be nigh tongue-tied. It comes close to scaring me stiff to make a speech. If ever I'm to have a good law practice or go up to the Legislature I've got to overcome my diffidence. And I don't know how."

Martitia spoke swiftly. "Why, Jonathan, you can't mean that truly. You sound so fine when you talk to us here at home. The night you came back I thought how grand your voice sounded and how beautiful the words you used to tell us about Hillsborough."

"It's middling easy to talk, sitting down, to one's own family. That's not like getting up on one's feet in a public place and expressing oneself to strangers. I was never one to use many words. I'm a quiet fellow."

"Yet always when you say something, Jonathan, it means a very great deal. I'm sure everybody else feels like I do about your speaking. 'Tisn't the large number of the words that count, but what they say."

"Before even one stranger, I always grow afraid of the sound of my own voice if I try to make a speech."

Martitia hesitated. "You didn't sound afraid of your own voice when you addressed that long speech to me as a stranger last summer at the Festival of the Dog. You sounded as though you enjoyed orating to me about Nantucket and the dogs of the Arctic and your Gardner ancestors."

Jonathan grinned. His face wore a puzzled look. "It's true that I was never afraid to make a speech or to use long sentences with you as a stranger when you first came to us. I don't know why that should be."

The girl was silent. She sat still, twisting one small hand meditatively over the other in her lap. Then she spoke with a rush: "If you were never afeared to make speeches to me as a stranger, Jonathan, maybe I could be of use in helping you to overcome your diffidence at speech-making to other strangers. Don't laugh at me when I tell you what I mean. It just came to me."

The young man looked at her, his face intent. "There's no laughter in me at you. I'd be grateful for any help you might will to give me."

"It's this. If you would pretend I was a whole audience of strangers instead of just one, and if you would practice speaking aloud your speeches to me, mightn't that help you to overcome your diffidence at public orating?"

The steady hazel eyes watching her grew bright. "It might help me, Martitia."

The little voice went on eagerly: "We could go outdoors each day at some time, and you could speak your speeches aloud to me, and I would sit very still and listen. I would smile or I would show you I disapproved just as someday your audiences will smile or disapprove when you go to the Legislature."

Jonathan reached out his long hand and touched Martitia's sleeve gently. "I don't think I've ever deserved that you should be kind to me. Since the first day that ever you came to Centre I've made your life miserable for you. Yet if you'll go with me each day and listen to my speeches I'll be grateful to you all of my life long."

The girl brushed one hand across her eyes. She spoke in a businesslike tone. "There's the mulberry orchard at the right of the hay barn where no one ever goes. It would make a fine place for speech-making. Shall we go there every day?"

"Yes, we'll go there every day this summer."

Suddenly the girl broke into a wavering smile. "I think I'll take along a ripe apple every time, and if I don't like your speech-making for the day I'll plop you with the ripe apple right in the chin."

Jonathan began to laugh. He kept on laughing helplessly. "You've grown to be almost a Gardner. If I don't mind out you'll be stealing a march on me like Pa or Addison would. I'll have to watch my step from now on."

Martitia rose from the steps. She smiled crookedly. "What I've learned about laughing, I learned from the

Gardners. 'Twill serve them right if I laugh back at one of them."

Addison appeared from the direction of the barn. He joined Martitia and his brother. "Where's Sandy, Martitia? This is the first time I've seen you without Sandy since Clarkson left."

"Doctor David borrowed Sandy from me to go round up a lamb for chops."

Addison turned to his brother. He winked solemnly. "Clarkson left Sandy with Martitia instead of taking him to Wilmington because Clarkson's in love with Martitia. Nothing else would have parted him from Sandy. Pa offered to get another sheep dog, but Clarkson refused to hear of taking Sandy with him."

Martitia ran up the steps toward the kitchen, but not before she caught a strange look on Jonathan's face. She pondered that look all the time she was helping Eunice with supper. What that look meant she could not figure.

Next afternoon late, when the field work for the day was over, Jonathan and Martitia set out for the mulberry orchard at the right of the hay barn.

Martitia looked up at the young man beside her on the path. She spoke with surprise. "I always forget how tall you are or how little I am till I walk along beside you like this. When I walk with Clarkson he doesn't tower so above me. Yet when I came to Centre all of you boys looked about the same to me."

Again Martitia caught that odd look on Jonathan's face. He was silent a while before he answered: "I wonder if there are not other deeper ways in which we Gardner boys look different to you now that you know us well?"

Martitia watched him in a puzzled fashion. "What do

you mean? Of course all of you boys are different. Addison is excitable. Barzillai is thoughtful. You are intellectual. Milton is a mixture of everybody. And Clarkson is the most gentle."

"You miss Clarkson, don't you?"

"Yes, I miss Clarkson. The house doesn't seem the same without him here to smile at us all."

"Clarkson is the handsomest Gardner. He has the warmest heart of any of us. He'll make a success in business down at Wilmington. They don't come any better than Clarkson."

The girl smiled. "That's queer, but Clarkson spoke almost the same words about you. It was long ago when I first came to Centre and went with him to salt the sheep. You Gardner brothers seem to love each other very much."

Jonathan's mouth clamped itself together. "Yes, we Gardner brothers stand together. We always will."

He changed the subject with abruptness. "At first, when I rehearse speeches to you, I'll memorize other men's words. Then later I'll use my own thoughts. I've decided to recite aloud to you today the Farewell Address of the father of this country. I memorized it last night and this morning while I was plowing. I'd like to rehearse, with proper gestures, the entire address; but especially that part where Mr. Washington warns us to 'frown upon the first dawning of any attempt to alienate any portion of our country from the rest.' There are those in this country who would attempt to prevent the operation in one state of the laws of the whole United States. If ever I am privileged to enter politics I shall make the preservation of this Union of States my polar star." Jonathan struck his hands together sharply.

Martitia's eyes shone. "Assuredly you will be in the Legislature someday, and you will help make laws that will keep the Union strong." She threw back her head.

Jonathan's eyes started twinkling. "You sound like a politician yourself. I believe you'd like to run for the Legislature against me. In that case, my constituents wouldn't vote for me in Guilford County. They'd prefer a pretty blue-eyed legislator to a lean, lantern-jawed fellow like me."

Martitia looked down. "I couldn't ever be ambitious for myself. I could only be ambitious for someone else. Here we are at the mulberry grove."

They entered the grove of mulberry trees. It was green and cool there. After the warmth of the late afternoon sun the coolness felt grateful to the girl's cheeks. She stared up at the trees. There must be thirty or forty of them, she guessed. Their white berries were luxuriant.

"Are these trees old, Jonathan?

"Most of them were here when Pa bought this land in 1800. Some have sprouted since. I've heard it said that someone planted them here to feed silkworms with. That sounds queer. They're handsome, though. And they form a fine roof for my legislature while I make speeches here."

Martitia settled herself on the ground under the larg-est mulberry tree of all. Jonathan stood before her. He began to speak somewhat awkwardly. Presently, however, his voice gathered more assurance. He threw back his shoulders and extended both hands when he came to the words: "Frown upon the first dawning of any attempt to alienate any portion of our country from the rest."

Martitia leaned forward to listen. Her mouth curved softly.

CHAPTER XVII

A Trip to Jamestown

THE BIG SPIDER that had built its web in the largest mulberry tree in the grove seemed to grow used to the comings and goings of a small girl in blue and a tall young man with a deep voice. Martitia, who watched the spider each day, wondered if the spider noticed how increased was the ease with which Jonathan spoke his thoughts aloud by the time June had merged imperceptibly into July. It seemed to Martitia that the big spider extended his web a little closer to the accustomed spot where Jonathan always stood. Motionless, as though intently listening, too, the spider hung in the air on its web and watched the tall young man extend his hands in larger and larger ease of gesture. The spider sometimes seemed to Martitia to tremble a little in excitement, as did also she, when Jonathan's voice vibrated more successfully than usual in expounding an imaginary legal situation or in pleading a fictitious case at the bar of the mulberry orchard.

It was with a sigh of regret at the prospect of three

speech-makings lost with Jonathan and the now-educated and doubtless legal-minded spider that Martitia took her part in the final plans in mid-July for going over to Jamestown to fetch Milton home and to visit the remarkable Sarah Gardner Mendenhall in her father's house.

Ruth elected to stay with the Macys. Addison remained behind to superintend the hired Quaker hands. The rest of the Gardner family set out early on the appointed morning, headed for Jamestown, ten miles away. Eunice held the reins in the gig, with Martitia at her side. Jonathan and Dr. David rode horseback. Sometimes Dr. David and Jonathan cantered their horses ahead of the gig; sometimes they dropped behind in earnest talk together. Often, in sheer exuberance of spirits, Jonathan would gallop his bay mare round and round the gig and its occupants, to the sad confusion of Eunice's white horse who drew the two-wheeled cart.

They came into Jamestown long before noon. Martitia watched the two-story houses on either side of the street. Eunice pointed out a handsome two-story house with brick chimneys. It stood on a corner.

"Yon place is Doctor Madison Lindsay's house where Milton dwells. Jamestown is a fine old settlement, founded by our kinsman, James Mendenhall. There are all of two hundred and fifty folk in Jamestown. We will stop now and greet Milton before we go on to Cousin Abel Mendenhall's."

They drew up at the handsome house on the corner. A hatless masculine figure catapulted suddenly from inside. The figure descended upon the visitors with loud war whoops. Martitia recognized Milton Gardner.

"Howdy, Pa. How are you, Ma? Is that a little merino lamb you've got by the side of you in the gig, Ma?"

Without waiting for an answer Milton hurled himself toward Jonathan who had got down swiftly from his mare at the side of the road. Ardently the two long-separated brothers greeted each other. Martitia felt a sharp thrust of jealousy. Jonathan's glowing face left her completely outside of his happiness at rejoining Milton.

Presently Eunice spoke. "We must be gone toward Cousin Abel's house, David. 'Tis nigh dinnertime. Sarah will not relish our keeping her pies and meat joints waiting. Sarah never keeps other folks waiting on her own doings."

They bade Milton a temporary good-by and rode on. The nearness of her inescapable meeting with Sarah Gardner Mendenhall, the paragon of Jamestown, weighed down Martitia's spirits. She made a face privately at the horse's tail. Then they approached Abel Mendenhall's place.

A young woman came swiftly from the brick house as they drove up. She was tall, Martitia noted bitterly, almost as tall as Jonathan. She had a quantity of neat blonde hair plaited around her head. She walked with the graceful motion of a woods' animal.

At sight of her Jonathan and Dr. David swung down from their horses. Jonathan strode to meet her in the brick path. He reached out a strong hand and wrung the almost equally powerful hand of Sarah Gardner Mendenhall. Martitia could hear their warm-noted voices. It seemed that Sarah's voice almost equaled Jonathan's in its quiet strength.

"Welcome, Cousin Jonathan."

"Twice a greeting to you, Cousin Sarah."

Martitia muttered something in her throat.

Eunice looked startled. "Did thee say aught to me, Martitia? It sounded as though thee said: 'I wish I had an apple.' Why should thee wish an apple now? 'Twill soon be dinnertime, and thee can eat to thy heart's content."

Martitia answered swiftly: "I said naught, Aunt Eunice."

Eunice got down from the gig. Martitia followed her. They went toward Sarah. At close range Martitia saw what Grandfather Daniel had meant by saying: "Sarah is a trifle plainer in looks than I fancy myself."

Sarah had a high, intelligent forehead and beautiful brown eyes. But her nose supplanted everything else in her face, Martitia noted. It was a large, masculine nose. Somewhat like the nose of dear, dead Mr. Washington himself in the picture that Jonathan kept, thought Martitia. Yes, Sarah Gardner Mendenhall's nose looked exactly like Mr. George Washington's nose!

Martitia cast a relieved glance at Jonathan. Then she felt her heart drop to the bottom of her copper-toed shoes. Jonathan was staring at Sarah in open admiration as she spoke to Eunice and Martitia.

"Thee is more welcome than I can tell thee, Aunt Eunice. And thee is welcome also, Martitia. Long have I wished to know the new little adopted cousin at Centre. Milton has told us many quaint tales of thy struggles with the loom and the breadboard. Thee must watch me at the loom while thee tarries with Pa and the children and me. Thee can adopt my new pattern of plaid woolen cloth. I learned it from the French lady who came to Jamestown to live by Deep River three years ago."

Martitia felt the color flood her slim cheeks. She

twitched her small, straight nose. Irresistibly she drew herself up to her entire five feet and shook back the dark cloud of her hair. Her heavy-lidded blue eyes shone mutinously.

"Thank you kindly, Sarah; I shall be glad in exchange to teach you my own invented pattern of star-shaped woolen twill. I invent my own patterns."

Sarah looked surprised. Martitia glanced quickly at Jonathan. She could not be sure whether his chin twitched a fraction or not. He did not waver in his admiring scrutiny of Sarah Gardner Mendenhall's face.

"Did Milton give you the Latin book of poems I sent you by him, Cousin Sarah?"

Sarah answered happily: "Milton gave me the Latin book, Cousin Jonathan. I have almost memorized the entire volume this winter. We will talk of it when dinner is done."

She turned to Eunice. "Come into the house now, Aunt Eunice. And thee also, Uncle David." She put out her hand to Dr. David with grave sweetness. "Pa couldn't come out to greet thee. Pa is too stiff with his rheumatism. Since Ma left us, Pa never seems to rally his old health and spirit again."

They went inside.

Martitia looked increasingly unhappy as the day wore on in Abel Mendenhall's house. The sight of Sarah gently deferring to her rheumatic and widowed father, the beautifully tended appearance of the four younger brothers and sisters whose motherless state Sarah quietly oversaw, was almost more than Martitia could bear. No wonder Jonathan did not mind a large nose where such capability and sweetness and intelligence were united! Sarah superintended the serving of a fine dinner of chicken and dumplings and pole beans and many elegant relishes. Martitia nearly choked on the flaky half-moon apple pies of Sarah's own making. Out in the kitchen was a hired servant, the Virginia girl knew; but it was Sarah's consummate skill and gracious handling that made the Quaker household of Abel Mendenhall move like the well-oiled Nantucket clock on the wall. Martitia grew paler and paler as the day went by.

Before supper Sarah took the little visitor up to the room where she kept her loom. Sarah exhibited such intricate and marvelous patterns of weaving that Martitia sat wordless.

"Tomorrow I will take thee to the French lady's house by Deep River and let her show thee how she weaves silk threads into cloth. The French lady, Madame de la Brousse, is very remarkable. She raises the silkworms herself and reels the silk from the cocoons. Then she weaves the threads into rich silken patterns. If I were not a true Friend I should secure a silk dress of her weaving."

Martitia answered dispiritedly: "I should like to see the French lady's silk weaving."

"Thee will not be able to understand Madame de la Brousse's French language. When I go there I must confer with her by gesture mostly. Madame has never learned much of our English tongue."

A small gleam lighted Martitia's face. "I can speak the French language, Sarah."

Sarah looked astounded. "But thee knows no Latin, Martitia. Milton says thee is not a learnèd female. How shouldst thee know the French tongue?"

"My mother's grandmother was French. My mother taught me French when I was a child. My mother had several French ladies for friends in Richmond."

Sarah appeared respectful for the first time that day.

The two girls rejoined the family downstairs. Milton came in from Dr. Lindsay's. It seemed to Martitia that Milton and Jonathan both went out of their way to converse with Sarah. It appeared from their talk that Sarah was a graduate of a female institute. She seemed to know as much as, or more than, the young men did about books and politics and world affairs. Martitia, who knew very little about world happenings or politics, listened silently while Jonathan and Sarah criticized President Andrew Jackson and praised Mr. Henry Clay. Jonathan admired Mr. Henry Clay passionately.

Martitia went forlornly to bed that night in one of Sarah Gardner Mendenhall's immaculate and handsome bedrooms. She said her prayers sadly by the tall fourposter where Eunice had already settled herself. Once in bed, she turned and tossed. She could not keep from seeing Jonathan's eyes sparkling at Sarah as Sarah had praised Mr. Henry Clay.

Next day Martitia and the other Gardners and Sarah spent the day with Cousin George Mendenhall in his handsome brick-chimneyed house. Martitia was taken by Dr. David to witness Cousin George's hundred black slaves working in his tanyard and smithy and carpenter's shop.

"You needn't to think that Cousin George, who is a true Friend, countenances slavery, Martitia." Dr. David explained the matter to Martitia with earnestness. "Cousin George, like Yearly Meeting of Friends itself in North

Carolina, secures slaves in order to teach them an honest trade. Then he sends them to Indiana and Iowa to be freed. In North Carolina freed Negroes may not live unless the state itself has freed them."

Martitia looked confused.

Dr. David pinched her cheek. "You are too pretty to understand large questions like slavery, child. It takes learnèd females like Sarah to think on such matters. But between you and me, I like females to be handsome rather than intellectual. Sarah's nose is too large."

Martitia felt comforted. She stayed close to Dr. David till afternoon. Jonathan appeared immersed in endless discussions with Sarah of the new Whig party and the new governor of North Carolina, Governor Swain.

In the afternoon Sarah prepared to take Martitia over by Deep River to inspect the French lady's silk weaving.

"I've a mind to go with you two," said Jonathan. "I'll drive the gig."

So Jonathan drove. Martitia had to sit on Sarah's lap. Sarah talked brilliantly and learnedly all the way to Madame de la Brousse's. Jonathan seemed to have grown silent once more. They entered a fine grove of mulberry trees at Sarah's direction.

"Here is Madame de la Brousse's," announced Sarah.

They climbed out of the gig. Sarah knocked at the house among the mulberry trees. A silk-clad lady came to greet them at the door.

Sarah addressed her loudly, as though Madame de la Brousse were deaf instead of a foreigner and might understand very loud English. "Madame, I have brought my two cousins from Centre to witness thy weaving of silk and thy culture of the silkworm. May we come in and observe thee at thy weaving, and may we witness thy silk-reeling women at their work also?"

The little lady extended both hands in unmistakable welcome, but she spoke softly in French: "*Je ne peux pas comprendre,* Mademoiselle Sarah. *Mais je vous donne la bienvenue.*"

Martitia answered in soft, precise French: "Forgive us our temerity, madame. My adopted cousin and I have come visiting our cousin Sarah Mendenhall in Jamestown. We wish greatly to observe you weave silk threads at the loom. Will you do us the incomparable honor of permitting us to come into your home and to witness your silk weaving?"

Jonathan's mouth fell slightly open. But Madame de la Brousse reached out both arms and caught Martitia close. She kissed her on each cheek. She broke into rapid French: "Dear child, you speak my own tongue. I have not heard my own tongue spoken correctly in three years. You speak it softly and prettily. For your knowledge of French I will show you everything I own. Come inside! You shall see my precious silkworm eggs even. You shall see everything, from egg to silken cloth on the loom."

Madame de la Brousse took Martitia's small fingers and held them tightly as she led the visitors about her home. Martitia watched and listened in enchantment. Like a piece of Dresden china was Madame de la Brousse. Like a fairy-tale house was the house among the mulberry trees.

Madame brought forth first from a cellar a little box which she unsealed carefully. She displayed some infinitesimal yellow-brown dots. "These are my French silkworm eggs. Out of these eggs come the silkworms themselves each spring. In six weeks the magic worms convert my mulberry leaves into rich silk cocoons. From mid-April to mid-May I tend the hatching and feeding of the worms. Come witness my sheds where I rear my worms each year. They are empty now, for the season of hatching is over till next April."

Madame de la Brousse led Martitia and the others to some low sheds at the back of her place. She pointed a delicate finger at the long tables and trays ranged neatly inside.

"On these flat tables and trays I keep my worms. Thirty days it requires to fatten the insects. Each day I must feed them great quantities of fresh mulberry leaves from my trees outside. They grow and they grow. Then they spin their cocoons at the month's end. By late May it is all done. I smother the moths inside the cocoons with heat. Then the rest of the year my reeling women reel the silk threads from the cocoons. Come witness my silk-reeling women at their work."

Martitia and Jonathan and Sarah went with the excitable French lady to a large room downstairs in her home. There three women sat with pans of warm water in front of them. In the water lay many cocoons to soak. Deftly the women caught from the pans the ends of silk thread and reeled them endlessly on to sticks.

"I can sell for currency all the pounds of raw silk thread I can muster each year," said Madame to Martitia in her quick French. "I secure five dollars in currency for each pound of the raw silk from my cocoons. Some silken cloth I weave also on my loom upstairs. It is a fine business, this silk culture, and amazingly simple. All you need are mulberry trees, a few ounces of silkworm eggs, some tables or trays, six weeks of warm springtime weather, common sense, and hard work. The government of your United States encourages vastly the growing of silk among its citizens now. I receive many pamphlets from them on how to improve my culture."

Martitia's blue eyes shone when Madame de la Brousse led her visitors upstairs to the loom where she was weaving silk cloth. Martitia looked at the pretty blue silk unfolding its warp and weft on the loom.

"Someday, madame," she vowed, "I shall weave a web of blue silk cloth also if I am ever rich enough to own the silk threads. To weave such magic threads would be like playing the keys of the spinet and making music with my fingers."

"You play the spinet, little one?" Madame's face beamed.

"I have not practiced in over a year. But once my mother taught me to play her own spinet well. That spinet is packed up in dusty wrappings over in Randolph County now."

"Come to my parlor and play for me now. I have a French spinet of my own mother's downstairs."

Martitia went down to the parlor. She settled herself shyly in front of the ivory keys. She felt Jonathan's eyes upon her. Madame de la Brousse and Sarah sat very still. Martitia shook back her dark hair and played. She played for her mother's unlistening ears to listen to now. She sang the words softly as she played: "Believe Me, If All Those Endearing Young Charms." By the time her small, true soprano had reached the lines: "Oh, the heart that has truly loved never forgets, But as truly loves on to the close," Martitia had forgotten her hearers here in the room. She woke with a start to the present once more.

She looked up from the keys. Jonathan was staring at her intently.

Madame de la Brousse clapped both her hands. Sarah sat silent. Martitia rose. "We must go, madame. We have trespassed too long on your hospitality. You have been an angel for kindness."

Madame de la Brousse would scarcely let Martitia go home at all. "I have not so enjoyed an afternoon in three years. To hear my own tongue so sweetly spoken in this alien land gives me a joy you cannot understand, child. I shall not soon forget you. If ever you wish a favor of Cécile de la Brousse only send word from Centre and ask it. If you were a silk culturist I would give you an ounce of my precious French silkworm eggs for your own. If you were a silk culturist I would buy all your cocoons of silk and pay you fifty cents a pound in currency for them. Since you are not a silk culturist, I must content myself with giving you three kisses on each cheek instead. Do not forget me. Come again and play my spinet for me."

She kissed Martitia good-by. As the gig drove away Madame de la Brousse called after Martitia in French: "When you marry I will send you a blue silk dress for your wedding."

Jonathan broke the silence of the afternoon. "What did the Frenchwoman say to you in good-by then, Martitia?"

Martitia turned crimson. "Nothing important."

Sarah began to talk brightly of a new book. She did not once mention Mr. Henry Clay or the Whig party on the way home. Jonathan concentrated his attentions on driving the horse.

Next morning the Gardners left Jamestown at sunup. Martitia did not see what farewell took place between

Sarah Gardner Mendenhall and Jonathan. The little Virginian said good-by to Cousin Abel and the children and Sarah inside. Then she turned her back on the family and went out alone to the waiting gig first of all the departing visitors.

On the trip back to Centre, Martitia said almost nothing. Her lips drooped. Once she caught the end of a discussion going on between Jonathan and Milton, whose horses followed close behind the gig.

"Yes, Sarah has a fine mind, Jonathan," said Milton. "But don't you agree with me that she talks too much? Sarah is very enlivening for a time. But say what you will about her fine mind and talents, she talks too much. Clarkson says Sarah's got a bell clapper instead of a tongue. I prefer Clarkson's taste for a gentle, pretty female like Martitia."

Martitia could not catch Jonathan's reply. Eunice began to talk at that moment. The girl swallowed a great lump in her throat. She could not compete with a paragon like Sarah Gardner Mendenhall for Jonathan! Sarah Gardner Mendenhall knew all about Mr. Henry Clay!

When they reached the house at Centre, Jonathan jumped down to help his mother and Martitia from the gig. As he lifted Martitia down by her elbows he held on to her firmly for a moment when her feet reached the ground. His eyes twinkled. He spoke to her softly: "Thee doesn't truly know how to weave an invented star-shaped pattern of woolen twill cloth on thy loom as thee told Sarah Gardner Mendenhall, does thee, Martitia?"

"No, Jonathan."

"I thought thee was lying a little bit, Martitia."

CHAPTER XVIII

Randolph versus Gardner

"DON'T THEE BE AFEARED of thy uncle James and his fine lawyer today in the courtroom, Martitia. All will be well with thee since David and Jonathan are there. And see that thee eats a good dinner in Greensborough before thee sets out for home this afternoon."

"Yes, Aunt Eunice."

Martitia squeezed herself into the gig between Jonathan and Dr. David. Eunice stood on the steps of the house with the sunlight of an August dawn softening her rugged face. Martitia waved to her as long as she could look back at the house among the pines and poplars. Dear house! Dear Quaker lady upon the steps!

Dr. David and Jonathan talked across Martitia's head.

"By Uncle James's letter I reckon that he and his precious lawyer are at the finest lodging-place in Greensborough. We will likely not see them till the case is called."

"Pa, you must bide today in court by the directions given you by Lawyer Peesley. I wish I had already been

licensed to practice and could plead Martitia's guardianship case with my own lips. But at least the preparation
of the whole matter has been mine. Lawyer Peesley is
only the mouthpiece of Jonathan Gardner this day."

"Being a Friend, I don't like the smell even of a courtroom, Son. It's strange a child of mine should hanker so
after the profession of lawyering."

"Maybe I'm not a Friend in fact, Pa. To be a Friend by
birth doesn't signify a Friend for life. I've never professed
the faith of a Friend. Maybe I'll join with the Presbyteri-
ans."

Jonathan stared straight ahead of him and did not
meet Martitia's quick glance that she threw up at him.

Dr. David sighed a little. "Your mother is the only
strict Friend of us all now. Since your grandfather
passed on and since your elder sisters went to Indiana
the Gardner household follows many of this world's
ways. Yet I've always felt that to be gentle in one's heart
is what makes a Friend more than the plain language
on one's lips."

Martitia listened to Dr. David's voice and no longer
heard what he said. Over and over in her head went the
dreadful thought: "This day I must meet Uncle James
and his lawyer in the court of Guilford. This day I must
know whether I am to leave Guilford County forever or
whether I am to be a Gardner daughter."

"How far will it be to Greensborough, Doctor David?"

"A matter of twelve miles, Martitia. We'll be at the
court by nine o'clock, starting as early as we have. Lawyer Peesley thinks our case will be called early on the
docket."

Martitia sat silent after that, hardly registering the

men's talk across her bent head. Once she heard Jonathan ask:

"Have you got the amount of surety for the guardianship bond with you, Pa?"

"I've got the surety, Son."

The rest of the trip was a blur to her. The coming into Greensborough, the sight of the courtroom, the faces of the lawyers and the witnesses and the magistrate: they were like pictures in the pages of a picture book to Martitia. In all the world there were only two things real to her: Uncle James's cool voice in greeting and Jonathan's hand on her arm in reassuring comfort. She looked bewilderedly from face to face as the legal words filled the room. Neither head nor tail could she make of the whole matter.

One question alone consumed her brain: "Will Uncle James's lawyer convince the court of Guilford that Uncle James instead of Doctor David is my true guardian? Or will Jonathan convince the court of Guilford through Lawyer Peesley that Doctor David and not Uncle James is fittest man to make me his ward?"

On and on went the arguments of the two lawyers. Martitia felt that she was no longer a real girl in a blue dress and bonnet, but merely a picture in a great legal book called *Randolph versus Gardner.* On another page of the book was Uncle James leaning forward with his chin on his slim patrician hand. Across from him was a picture of the two red-faced lawyers. Beyond that was a picture of Dr. David, handsome but unsmiling. On the cover of the book was a great picture of the magistrate himself. And turning the pages of the book was Jonathan's own hand, familiar and long-fingered and strong.

Martitia heard the magistrate's voice begin rendering the court decision at last. The great legal book was closing. Jonathan's hand had turned the final page.

"As the Court have a discretional power in chusing the most proper person for guardianship of an orphan, they should make their election of that person who can best attend to the affairs of the orphan, and whom they have reason to believe will attend to them with the greatest advantage and most fidelity to the orphan. Mr. Randolph is stated to live at the distance of three or four hundred miles in another state. Should he be appointed guardian he must either carry the ward with him to his place of residence, where the Court cannot from time to time be informed of his treatment; or he must leave the ward in the possession of an agent. Mr. Gardner, on the other hand, resides on the spot, near to the orphan's estate. Should he mismanage, intelligence may immediately be conveyed to the Court.

"Moreover, Mr. Gardner has no prospect of ever succeeding to the ward's estate through kinship. Whereas Mr. Randolph by kinship has. Mr. Gardner might, therefore, be presumed by the Court to have no remote reason whatever for not preserving the life and person of the orphan.

"Wherefore let Mr. Gardner be appointed."

Martitia turned to Jonathan. "Oh, Jonathan, Jonathan, you've won your first case! I shall be a Gardner daughter!"

Jonathan smiled down at her.

In a jumble of happiness she saw Dr. David give bond and securities for her guardianship, as the act of the State of North Carolina required.

Uncle James conceded honest defeat with a cool, polite

good-by to Martitia and Dr. David and Jonathan. Then Martitia went with the Gardner men to the nearest inn and dutifully tried to eat dinner as Eunice had bade her to do. The three of them glowed.

Then she climbed into the gig between Jonathan and Dr. David. Still in a joyful daze she watched the corn-fields fade backward on either side. Soon the Gardner house would come in sight around a bend in the dusty road. The Gardner house! Her own house also now!

There showed the house through the poplar trees and pines. And there on the steps in the sunset light stood Eunice. Dear house! Dear Quaker lady upon the steps!

Martitia fled up the yard when they climbed from the gig. Eunice's arms went out to meet her.

"Welcome, Daughter. I know by thy face that all is well. My son Jonathan has won his case. Did I not tell thee this dawn that naught could go ill with thee when David and Jonathan were at thy side?"

Martitia lifted a wet face from Eunice's shoulder. She saw the little woman's eyes go past her and beyond. She watched those indomitable lips form soundlessly the three words:

"My son Jonathan."

CHAPTER XIX

Greater Love Hath No Man

"THIS IS THE LAST TIME I shall make a speech to you in the mulberry orchard till next summer, Martitia. Do you suppose a descendant of this summer's spider will watch us again next year when I come back?"

"Perhaps you won't want to rehearse speeches with me then, Jonathan."

"I'll always want to rehearse speeches with you."

"Jonathan, will you tell me something if I ask it of you?"

"I reckon I will. What is it?"

"Is Doctor David having a hard time to keep the farm going now? He looks worried. Do tell me what it is. A Gardner daughter should share the Gardner sorrows as well as the Gardner joys."

Jonathan hesitated. "Pa worries some. With Barzillai and Clarkson gone he has to pay the two extra hired hands. Money's never plentiful with Pa. Patients are supposed to pay once a year for the doctoring Pa does. But

194

many folks don't or can't pay. Pa depends mostly on the farm. And the grain crops are bad this year."

Martitia sighed. "I wish I was more use to Doctor David. I'm a trouble to him, too, another person to feed and clothe. And Doctor David will never let my rents from the house in Asheborough go to my upkeep here. He says I'm his own daughter. He says my rents must be kept for me as a marriage portion."

Jonathan looked away. "Have you had letters from Clarkson, Martitia?"

"Yes, Clarkson sent me separate letters both times that he wrote by the post to his father and mother. The letters to me were much like the letters to Doctor David and Aunt Eunice. Why do you ask me?"

"I only wished to know."

"Clarkson sent me a pretty trinket, too, a coral brooch which he said he bought from one of the schooners from Havana." Martitia's face shadowed. " 'Twas a strange coincidence. I had another brooch and lost it the day before Clarkson went away. It was a miniature that my mother painted of me. I wore it to the wood's lot to help salt the sheep with Clarkson, and I lost it somehow on the way back. I could never find it, no matter how I searched."

Jonathan spoke slowly: "You and Clarkson are somewhat alike. You are both full of gentleness and quaint fancies. I reckon you have a great deal in common?"

"Yes, a great deal in common."

Jonathan shook his shoulders. "They don't come any finer than Clarkson. He deserves the best in all of this world. And if I have anything to do with it, he shall have it."

The girl looked at him curiously. "You sound as

though you were signing away your rights to a future fortune."

"Maybe I am."

The young man rose abruptly. He looked a little white and weary. "I'll speak my speech and we'll go back to the house. I've enough of the stifling air in the mulberry orchard for this year. It's like to choke me here."

Martitia got up with a flounce. "Well, if that's the way you feel about your speech-making with me in the mulberry orchard I'm sorry you didn't tell me before. We'll go without waiting for today's speech. I reckon it takes a female with knowledge of Latin and Mr. Henry Clay and the Whig party to make a man forget the simple heat of a September afternoon."

Jonathan did not answer. He followed her back to the house in silence.

Next day he left Centre for Hillsborough. No further words passed between him and Martitia in private. He told her good-by before all the rest of the family and went away on horseback. He would not be home again till he had completed Mr. Bingham's school courses in June. The house seemed infinitely empty to Martitia with his going. Eunice looked uncommonly grave.

With the coming of October Milton set forth to practice medicine with his mother's relatives in Asheborough. A winter of study with Dr. Lindsay had prepared him better than most young doctors. Only Addison remained at home now.

"I'm going to stay with you always, Pa," said Addison when Milton rode away. "You've given three sons their horses to take with them when they went to try their fortunes in the world. You need one farmer son to stay at home with you. Jonathan will come home in June. But he'll only tarry a few weeks till he sets out once more for Judge Debow's house to read law. Then he'll set up his shingle in Asheborough, too, like he's always planned. He'll marry Sarah maybe. And Milton will wed some Randolph County girl. That's the last we'll see of them except for visits. I'll be your farmer son, Pa."

Dr. David answered slowly: "I need you, Son. I'm glad you've got no hankering to go forth and leave me. I miss my sons."

Martitia, who was standing near, came close and slipped her hand into Dr. David's. "You've got another daughter, sir."

The big man's face lightened. "That's true, child. Come with me and watch me salt the sheep. You used often to go with my son Clarkson when he did it."

Martitia left Ruth and Eunice standing together on the porch. She went with Dr. David. Addison went off toward the barn.

All through the blue days of October and the gold beginnings of an unprecedentedly warm November Martitia contrived to stay a great deal with Dr. David. When she was not busy with her weaving she sat in his office and talked to him while he compounded his prescriptions for patients: salts and senna, calomel and jalap, Peruvian bark and dogwood bitters. She helped him pack his saddlebags with his medicines and his eternal lancet for bloodletting when he set out on sick calls. With the going of summer she noted how his almost unbroken summertime farming yielded to doctoring autumn ailments. It seemed to comfort Dr. David, in the loss of his sons about him, to have Martitia close.

One afternoon near the middle of November Martitia came up from her springhouse weaving. The day was beautifully sunny and full of late gold leaves on the trees. Frost, she thought, had been uncommonly late in stripping the leaves from the poplars. She remembered, looking at the yellow leaves, how Clarkson had said to her last May: "And will you write me letters next year to say how the poplar trees turn gold in the autumn, Martitia?"

She spoke to Sandy, who was forever at her heels: "This very night, Sandy, I will borrow the family quill and write to Clarkson and tell him how the poplar trees are still golden at Centre, though most of the leaves have fallen. I will ask him how the schooners from the Indies look in the river harbor at Wilmington. And I will tell him how I miss him always here at Centre. Since Jonathan likes only females of great intellect I shall perhaps tell Clarkson to hasten back home from Wilmington when May brings the maypops once more to the vines by the Meeting House. Clarkson is kind and handsome. He is gentlehearted, Sandy. His smile makes my throat grow tight." Martitia started singing a little song.

She left Sandy on the front porch and went into the kitchen, still humming her little tune as she entered. The tune died on her lips at sight of Dr. David and Eunice there. Across from the table they were sitting, a letter open and spread out on the cloth between them. White-lipped and silent they sat. Dr. David's great hand was stretched out across the table to cover Eunice's smaller, work-hardened fingers. Their eyes were fixed steadfastly on each other. They did not hear the girl enter.

She stood in an agony of fear at what dreadful news

could have so swiftly set the look of an old man upon Dr. David's face and could have twisted that powerful mouth of Eunice's into its look of incredible suffering. Martitia drew back to leave. Dr. David heard her at last. Without taking his eyes from Eunice he motioned his head toward the letter on the table.

"Take it and read it, Martitia."

Martitia hesitated, incapable for a minute of movement.

Dr. David spoke again. "Take it to your room and read it. Ruth and Addison already know."

The girl forced her fingers to lift the strewn sheets. She dared not look at Eunice. She fled from the kitchen and stumbled up the stairs. Once in her room, she sat at the window and held the letter in terrified fingers. It was impossible to read it at first. Then she shivered and set her eyes to trace the words. The handwriting on the closely lined sheets was unmistakably Barzillai's.

Duplin County,
North Carolina
Nov. 5, 1832

MY DEAR FATHER AND MOTHER,

It is now late at night. I have been awake since sunrise and am fully used up. Yet I must write you. I do not see how I am to tell you what I must. A great calamity has befallen us Gardners. Clarkson is no more. He has perished in a pestilential visitation of yellow fever, yielding up his life on November 1st while rendering succor to the ill and the dying. It is with a heavy heart I write you. I was not with him in Wilmington when he died. Having him gone overcomes me. Yet the more minute accounts I have had of his last hours cheer me and are of the most comforting character. He died with a good hope and repeating only a few moments before he expired the words of the psalmist, "Bless the Lord, oh my soul and all that is within me bless His holy name." I recite these particulars because they will be comforting to you as they surely have been to me.

And now let me explain to you, my dear father and mother, how all of this calamity overtook us. In September Clarkson and I were happily lodged at a house in Wilmington and working each day in Jethro Swain's warehouse. But in September yellow fever appeared in Wilmington, introduced by the brig John London *from Havana. It began to rage with great violence immediately. The family with whom we lodged, Clarkson and I, urged us to flee with them to a relative's home here in Duplin County to avoid the pestilence. I felt that such a course was only sensible to follow, since we were not physicians or nurses and could not be of certain use in aiding the sufferers. But Clarkson thought otherwise. He said he could not bear to leave the dying and the ill. Most of the town was fleeing to escape the dreadful and deathly pestilence. The streets were deserted, filled only with a black pall of smoke from the burning tar barrels designed to purify the air and mitigate the pestilence. The silence was broken only by the cries of the widows and orphans and by the rumbling of the funeral carts. I fled with the family with whom we lodged, bringing Reuben Swain with me, and came here to Duplin County. Clarkson, nobler than I, stayed behind, regardless of self, to minister to the wants of those who were unable to leave. Distributing food to the poor, medicine and attendance to the sick, consolation to the dying, and holy burial to the dead, he stayed behind when others fled. He nobly fulfilled his trust.*

My dear parents, I have but this day learned of my brother's death. A certain man who fled late from the stricken city of Wilmington bore the news to me this sunup. This man re-counted how when my brother passed on in his hand was found a miniature of a little girl with a blue ribbon on her hair. That miniature was buried with him. Clarkson lies now with the other yellow fever dead in the communal trenches at Wilmington.

My dear father and mother, I have written under unfavor-able circumstances and without connection no doubt. Reuben has this day also written to his parents that he is safe in Duplin County. We will return to Wilmington when the town is free of the plague once more. I hope I may be as ready to go as Clarkson was. There is a man here who has written in the papers of Clarkson and of those other heroic souls who stayed behind and perished with him: "Rest they well and rest they calmly; They need no monument above them; That is to be found in the hearts of those who knew them."

Your bereaved and saddened son,

BARZILLAI

Martitia sat dry-eyed, too shaken for any tears. Over and over she kept seeing Clarkson's mouth in its poign-ant curve of laughter. Never again would she see that mouth or hear it laugh in gentleness at her. Never again would she see those brilliant black eyes or that familiar toss of the dark head.

Oh, Clarkson, why did you go away in the May sunshine and leave Sandy and me crouching on the grass to watch you climb the hill and pass out of our sight forever? Why did you take my mother's miniature from my dress that day in the wood's path, to lie at last in the still hands that had minis-tered to the dying and the dead? Did you love the little girl

*with the blue ribbon on her hair? And did she comfort you at
the last? Undaunted, tenderhearted Clarkson; you would not
leave the dying alone to face their fate untended. I know how
it was with you. You were gentle to me also.*

Martitia got up from her chair blindly and went down
the steps to the front porch. Sunset reddened the sky
behind the poplar trees and pines. Sandy crouched on
the steps where she had left him an hour ago, or was it a
lifetime ago, or a hundred years ago? Martitia went to
the dog and knelt and gathered his brown head with its
faithful eyes to her heart.

"Your master isn't coming home to us, Sandy. Your
master will never come riding up to the Gardner house
when maypops are ripe by the Meeting House as he said
he would come. Oh, Sandy, Sandy!"

The dog whined. The girl buried her face in his neck.
Behind her she heard the faint sound of footsteps. She
raised her empty eyes to watch who came. Eunice moved
across the porch with that curiously light tread of hers,
almost like velvet. She came to the steps where Martitia
crouched. In the light of the failing November sun Eunice's
mouth looked so much like Jonathan's that Martitia almost cried out. Nor life, nor death, she thought; nor
things present, nor things to come, can break or perma-
nently bow that unwavering strength in those two indomitable mouths of mother and son: Eunice Gardner
and her son Jonathan. Eunice's eyes showed dark with
their suffering; but the powerful, thin lips clamped together. Only such a woman could produce such sons,
thought Martitia in her own frailty.

Eunice spoke. Her voice was dry but steady. "Daughter, go to my husband David and comfort him. He has

need of thee now. To Ruth and to me Divine Providence did not see fit to give the gift of tenderness as He richly gave it to thee and to David and to my son Clarkson." Over the phrase "My son Clarkson" Eunice's voice thinned out. She stopped abruptly. But in a moment she lifted her face toward the sunset sky.

"Flesh of my flesh, bone of my bone," she murmured. "He was my son."

Martitia saw the big-knuckled hands twist at her sides. But the steadfast voice went on: "Into whose hands might I commit my sons better than into those hands which have made heaven and earth? It is ill with me, but it is well with them."

She ceased speaking. In a moment she turned to the girl crouched on the steps. "Go to my husband David and comfort him, child. He needs thee."

Martitia got up and went to Dr. David.

CHAPTER XX

A Gardner Daughter

SNOWFALL SUCCEEDED snowfall at Centre. The barns were almost always peaked with the white masses of flakes through as unprecedentedly cold a December and January as the October and November had been unprecedentedly warm.

Martitia watched the snowflakes obliterate every line of fields and low bushes outdoors. Indoors she marked how the passing of the days fell like snowflakes to smooth out the lines of suffering in the Gardner faces. Life resumed something of its accustomed pattern of work and laughter. Sometimes, in the midst of her work in the kitchen, though, Martitia would see a listening look fall over Eunice's face. In a flash Martitia would find herself listening, too, certain that in a moment Clarkson's laughter would sound from the back porch. A quick hand would squeeze her breathless for a second. Then she would go on with her work, observing how Eunice also went on with her bread-making or her candle-molding. Less and less frequent were the recurrences of these sharp stabs by the time March broke upon Centre in a wild burst of wind that nearly bent the mulberry trees double.

On a morning in early March Martitia went with Addison and Dr. David to see a new calf, born the night before. She walked between the two men and listened to their talk.

"Son, you'll want to take every care of this calf. I can't afford to lose any more stock. Last year's loss of the lambs in that late cold spell reduced my fleeces. There's trouble enough already on hand without more to add to it." He sighed.

Martitia looked up at him quickly. "Doctor David, is there trouble on the farm?"

The big Quaker peered down at her. He smiled. "Don't worry your pretty little noodle over farming matters, child. Everything's all right."

The girl, unsatisfied, had to be content with his answer. But later, when Dr. David had gone back up to his office, Martitia questioned Addison closely. They stood in the barn.

"You and Doctor David and Ruth and Aunt Eunice are keeping something from me, Addison. I feel it in the air. Something very wrong is the matter with Doctor David and the rest of you lately. Do tell me what it is."

Addison whistled nonchalantly. "Didn't you hear Pa tell you to keep your little brown noodle out of this matter, Martitia? I've a mind to spank your little bottom good for trying to drain information out of me." Solemnly he turned Martitia over on one knee and started spanking her.

Martitia wriggled loose and went streaking out of the barn. The boy followed her, grinning.

"Until Jonathan comes home for good in June I'll have to keep you in order. You're getting too persnickety."

Martitia stared up at him. "What do you mean by saying 'When Jonathan comes home for good in June?' You know perfectly well that Jonathan's only going to stay home two weeks before going back to Judge De-bow's to read law in Orange County."

Addison appeared to be too intent on turning a som-ersault backward, all but landing in a tub of water set there for the stock, to answer. He said nothing.

Martitia looked frightened. "There's something wrong about Jonathan. I know it. Tell me quickly, Addison. I've got a right to know. I'm a Gardner daughter too."

Addison surveyed her redly. "I've already told too much with this loose-hinged tongue of mine. Let me alone now. I won't say another word."

"Yes, you will. I'll make you. If you refuse I'll go this minute and ask Doctor David what it's all about. That will be a worry to him. You'd rather tell me yourself than bother your father, wouldn't you?"

Addison looked increasingly unhappy. He scratched his nose; he cleared his throat, he wiggled his ears. Fi-nally he spoke dolefully: "Now that I've let the cat out of the bag I might as well spare Pa your questioning. He's sick to heart over this matter already. Come here and sit on the fence, and I'll tell you."

Martitia perched herself on the fence by him.

He began slowly. "It's like this, Martitia. Pa always aimed to have enough currency saved up for Jonathan to use in going to Judge Debow's to read law. 'Tisn't like going to school, as the boys went to Doctor Lindsay's or to Mr. Bingham's. There Pa could pay their tuition in farm produce. But at Judge Debow's Jonathan will have to carry good currency, enough for his lodging and up-keep and his fee to Judge Debow. Judge Debow is a rich man. He just elects to let a few extra-smart young men live near to his plantation and come over to read law with him at night and when he's not too busy with his judge-ship."

Addison paused a long time. Martitia said painfully: "Go on."

Addison went on. "Well, things have gone wrong with Pa's prosperity. Pa has had uncommon calls for currency and securities this year. He's had uncommon bad luck at farming. So you might as well know, Marti-tia, Pa's got to write Jonathan he'll have to give over going to Judge Debow's in June. Jonathan will have to wait at least until autumn, till Pa gets on his feet again. Maybe crops will be better in the fall."

Martitia put one hand to her throat.

Addison said with a deep sigh: "Jonathan's going to be disappointed beyond anything you or I could under-stand. He's waited longer than any of the rest of the boys to get his chance. Jonathan wouldn't desert Pa on the farm. He stayed home to render a son's full service till he was twenty-one. He's twenty-three now. He's deserving of his chance before he's any older. Every month counts to him now. Other men less smart than he is are already practicing law and going to the Legislature. Jonathan could have done it, too, if he'd been willing to desert Pa.

Now he's got to wait again." Addison's voice trailed off in misery.

Martitia stilled the trembling of her lip by catching it between her teeth. She took a deep breath. "One thing I must know, Addison. Did putting up bond and securities for my guardianship have anything to do with Doctor David's being short of currency?"

Addison stared downward. He appeared intent on kicking his shoe against the bottom fence rail. He refused to say a word in answer.

Martitia got down swiftly from the fence. "Since you won't answer, I'll go ask Doctor David."

Addison stopped her with a quick hand. "No, don't go asking Pa such questions. If you must know, I'll be the one to answer. Pa'd cut out his tongue before he'd make you party to this business. He sets more store by you than you know. It's not your fault, but making surety for your guardianship did straiten Pa's circumstances. That's not all, though. Bad crops did their part. And Pa had to let three sons go this year and give them their horses. The hired hands take money. You needn't to blame yourself for this trouble, Martitia."

"But if I hadn't come here Jonathan could have had his chance in June."

"Jonathan can wait till autumn. Jonathan's smart. He could wait ten years and still come out on top of every other man in this county. Jonathan's got brains."

The girl looked wanly at the boy. "Thank you for telling me. I've got to go think things out. Good-by."

She streaked off toward the house. On the front steps she sat down and thought. Presently she walked slowly over to Dr. David's office. He was treating a patient. Martitia had to wait outside. When the patient was gone Martitia went in. She faced Dr. David.

"It doesn't matter how I found out, sir, but I know about Jonathan and the Gardner trouble. I'm a Gardner daughter too. I had a right to know. I've come to offer some sort of solution. I've got forty dollars in currency upstairs in my trunk. You know, sir, it's what my father left. With that and with the thirty dollars in currency that have come in from Asheborough since you rented my father's small house there last August how long could Jonathan stay at Judge Debow's?"

"Sixty dollars of it would keep Jonathan in Orange County for three months, child. Maybe by then I'd be on my feet again. But the matter of your little capital or your rents isn't in question here. They are your own property, left you by your father. I couldn't touch them, Daughter."

At that word "Daughter" Martitia broke out joyfully: "Don't you see, sir? I'm a Gardner daughter too. You called me so. What is mine is the Gardners' also. Everything I have is theirs to use as their need requires. You let me weave cloth for the Gardners. Will you not let my property be theirs too?"

Dr. David reached over and patted Martitia's hand. "You are a dear daughter. No man ever had a gentler, prettier one. But I see I'll have to explain to you how a man's heart doesn't interfere with his rightful self-respect and pride. Your service as a daughter I gladly receive, as I do Ruth's. That is proper and even right. But your worldly possessions I cannot accept or even use temporarily. I administer them in trust for your father and under the supervision of the courts. When you come of age at twenty-one you must receive intact every penny accruing to you through these years of my guardianship. Let the matter of your money being used for Jonathan drop immediately. Thank you, child. But there can be no question of that. My son Jonathan would be the last to accept your aid. He is more proud than I even. Did you not ever inquire into that firm chin of his and those powerful lips?" Dr. David smiled as though to take the sting out of his words.

Martitia bowed her head over. She wept. She got her words out with difficulty. "I cannot bear, sir, to have Jonathan lose his chance to go to Judge Debow's this June when he wishes it so. Other things I could bear, but not this."

The big man stroked her head. "I was never sure before where your heart lay. Often last year I asked myself: 'Is it my stern son or my gentle son who possesses my new daughter's heart?' " Dr. David's face shadowed as he pronounced the words: "My gentle son."

He went on after a moment: "Has Jonathan said anything to you?"

Martitia answered almost in a whisper: "No sir."

Dr. David got up suddenly, shaking his great shoulders. "This is enough of sad matters for one day in March. Let us laugh and be glad, as the Lord meant us to be. Spring is coming. I saw pussy willows by Polecat Creek yesterday. And a new spider is spinning his web impudently across my window yonder. Come see him weave his marvelous silk."

The girl slowly got up and went to the window with

Dr. David. Truly enough, a spider had begun to trace his springtime geometry across the office window.

"That fellow there can make a finer web than you, child. He weaves silk instead of wool or cotton like you do. If you had silk threads you might match his magic."

Martitia watched the spider. She listened to Dr. David's words. Suddenly a gleam of pure excitement entered her eyes. She turned to Dr. David with a gasp. "Will you accept anything for Jonathan that I do with my own hands, sir?"

"I don't know whether I can speak for Jonathan. I can only speak for myself. But anything you do with your own hands I'll be glad to accept. Have you discovered a gold mine?"

Martitia refused to answer. She asked one more question. "Do you know anyone who is going over to Jamestown soon? Anyone who might take a message to someone there for me?"

"Christian Swain spoke of going three days from now. Don't tell me you like Sarah Gardner Mendenhall so well that you wish to send a message to her."

"No sir. It's not to Sarah I wish my message to go. It's to the French lady, Madame de la Brousse. Will you promise not to write to Jonathan yet to say that he is not to go to Judge Debow's in June?"

Dr. David looked puzzled. He agreed, however, to see that Christian Swain took Martitia's missive with him to Jamestown in three days. And he promised not to write to Jonathan yet.

Martitia went to her room and spent a long time inscribing her message. She took extra pains with the composition. Fortunately she knew that her French spelling was correctly taught her, unlike her less fortunate English spelling. As she wrote the letter she kept hearing the little Frenchwoman's words over and over in her ears: "I can sell for currency all the pounds of raw silk thread I can muster each year. It is a fine business, this silk culture, and amazingly simple. All you need is mulberry trees, a few ounces of silkworm eggs, some tables, six weeks of warm springtime weather, common sense, and hard work. If you were a silk culturist I would give you an ounce of my precious French silkworm eggs for your own. If you were a silk culturist I would buy all your cocoons of silk and pay you fifty cents a pound in currency for them. If ever you wish a favor of Cécile de la Brousse only send word from Centre and ask it."

When she took the letter over to put it into Dr. David's hands for safe-keeping until Christian Swain carried it to Jamestown, Martitia explained to Sandy, who accompanied her: "I'm asking the help from Madame de la Brousse which she offered, Sandy. I do pray hard that she truly meant what she said last summer and will answer soon."

Martitia paid a daily visit to the mulberry orchard at the right of the hay barn to inspect the appearance of potential buds on the boughs. "If I am to rear silkworms, Sandy," she told her collie dog, "I must have mulberry leaves to feed the insects with from mid-April to mid-May. That's what Madame de la Brousse said."

When Christian Swain came back from Jamestown he brought a packet addressed to "Mademoiselle Martitia Howland." Martitia could scarcely undo the wrappings in her excitement. Inside was a small, tightly sealed

box, a letter, and a pamphlet book. Martitia read the
letter first. It was in French.

> *Jamestown, North Carolina*
> *March 9, 1833*

My dear Little One,

*Gladly do I answer your request for instructions on silk
culture. And gladly will I buy whatever quantity of cocoons
you can arrange to send over to me when your worms are
hatched and have done with their rising. I am sending you an
ounce of my precious silkworm eggs. Do you contrive to make
fine use of them with your work and your mulberry trees. You
will secure, with good luck, about a hundred pounds of cocoons
when the chrysalids have been smothered. At fifty cents a
pound that will realize you fifty dollars in currency if you
send them over to me in Jamestown. To reel the silk from the
cocoons would bring you more returns, but the reeling requires
experience. My women can do it. I think that you would take
a year or more to learn how. So rest yourself with the cocoons
alone.*

*I am enclosing a new pamphlet from the government,
containing fullest directions in very simple form for the hatching and rearing and feeding of the worms. Take care to place
the box of eggs now in a cool, dry place till you are ready to
start hatching them about the middle of April. I am happy
that you have a fine mulberry grove close at hand. If you can
contrive to arrange your tables in a near-by barn or outhouse
all will be easy for you to handle alone. The last ten days of
feeding you will need someone to help with the work.*

*My dear child, can you not arrange to come over with your
cocoons and visit with me? To hear my own language cor-*

rectly spoken in a foreign land is refreshing. I send my love to you. Good luck. I shall look for the cocoons about the last of May; and I shall pray that you will come with them. May Providence bless you.

Your affectionate friend,

CÉCILE DE LA BROUSSE

Martitia climbed down into the winter cellar under the kitchen and deposited her little sealed box of silk-worm eggs where they would be safe till mid-April. Then she examined her pamphlet book. It bore the title:

A MANUAL

Containing

Information Respecting the Growth

of the

MULBERRY TREE

with

Suitable Directions

for the

CULTURE OF SILK

Boston

1833

After a week of careful study in the *Manual* Martitia addressed Sandy as she went down to her weaving at the springhouse: "I have the silkworm eggs, Sandy. I have the mulberry trees. I have the directions for the hatching and the rearing of the worms. Soon I shall have the six weeks of warm springtime weather. Then I must produce from inside myself the common sense and the hard work, as the worms will spin silk from their own insides. Doctor

David says I may have the great low tables in the hay barn for my rearing shelves to keep the worms while they eat the mulberry leaves and spin their cocoons. At any cost I must succeed. Doctor David says that if I make fifty dollars in currency he can raise the other ten dollars of currency to send Jonathan to Judge Debow's in June. Maybe in the fall the crops will be good again. Oh, Sandy, I *must* succeed! Jonathan mustn't be made to wait another season!"

CHAPTER XXI

The Magic Worm

"TOMORROW WE AIM to finish shearing the sheep, Martitia. Then the hay barn is yours to use for your silk culture." Dr. David spoke to Martitia in a businesslike tone.

The girl stopped eating her supper. She answered excitedly: "Day after tomorrow will be April fourteenth. The weather now is perfect for my worms. The new mulberry leaves are just right. I will take my silkworm eggs from the cellar day after tomorrow and expose them in the hay barn to hatch."

Addison interrupted: "I'll nail some rims around the tables for you, Martitia, so your worms will not fall off. Pa and I will push the shearing tables back against the wall of the barn. Later on, when you want more space for the growing worms, as your pamphlet book says, I'll set many extra planks between the tables to add more room. You'll have fine spaces for your worms."

"It worries me a little to think how many leaves I must pick from the mulberry orchard to feed my worms with as they grow. I shall have to work very hard for the next few weeks. Aunt Eunice, will you forgive me if I spend little time at my weaving till May is over?"

"I would forgive thee far more than that, Martitia, if thy silkworms give Jonathan his chance to go to Orange County as he plans in June. My husband has not told my son Jonathan that aught of change or uncertainty waits for him here when he returns. Thy worms mean much to all of the Gardners, not to thee alone."

Dr. David spoke again: "This morning I searched in the loft of the barn. I found there what I sought. It was a small wagon that my children had when they were lads and lasses. The wagon will serve to aid you in fetching the mulberry leaves from the orchard to the barn. With our large basket of split oak to set upon the wagon, you will be well prepared for many trips between orchard and barn. Because you are somewhat dwarfish and many of the mulberry trees are somewhat tall, I will contrive to set a ladder handy in the orchard for you to climb upon in picking your leaves."

Martitia clapped her hands. Addison looked at his father with concern. "Pa, your words just brought to my mind a dreadful thought about Martitia's small size. Do you reckon that Martitia is really a dwarf, being so under-sized? Is it likely that Martitia is a dwarf of some malicious variety who will set an evil spell upon the Gardners some dark of the moon? I'm afeared of Martitia and her dwarfish size that can't reach up to even a low mulberry tree's boughs with ease."

Martitia began to laugh. Addison got up from the table and turned two somersaults backward.

Ruth looked at him coldly. She addressed Martitia: "It

appears to me that the whole idea of your raising silkworms is of a piece with Addison's somersaults and foolish
words. It's plain nonsense. You've got an ounce of that
French lady's silkworm eggs to start with. I looked at that
pamphlet book of yours, and it said on page 35 that one
ounce of eggs will produce forty thousand worms who
consume one thousand pounds of leaves to produce about
one hundred pounds of cocoons. Now you know that no
one as small and weak as you are, Martitia, can tote a
thousand pounds of leaves from the orchard to the barn."

Martitia stiffened. She stared into Ruth's eyes across
the table. That old antagonism of the strong for the weak
was still working like yeast in Ruth's independent ego!
During the long hard months of effort at the loom and
in the kitchen Martitia had grown to believe that Ruth
was beginning to respect her. Yet here was the old con-
tempt still alive.

Martitia spoke clearly: "I may be small, and I may
have small hands, but I can tote a thousand pounds of
leaves easily. I can tote *ten* thousand pounds of leaves if
necessary. I can tote *twenty* thousand pounds of leaves. I
can . . ."

Addison interrupted: "Stop, Dwarf. You'll be toting
the Gardner house off its foundation if someone doesn't
stop you."

He turned to his sister. "The thousand pounds of
leaves is spread out over the whole thirty-two days required to raise the worms after they hatch. Besides, I'm
going to help Martitia with the leaf-toting during the
last ten days when those worms get to eating too much
for one person to handle. I can spare a few hours a day
from the fields. Pa's already agreed to it."

Martitia thanked Addison with her eyes.

Ruth looked disgusted. "Every tub ought to stand on its own bottom."

Two mornings later Martitia surveyed her domain in the hay barn. She saw with delight how well the barn fulfilled the requirements for silk culture as outlined in her pamphlet book. Here was a nice dry floor and large doors for ventilation. Addison had pushed the big sheep-shearing tables back against the wall.

With great care Martitia unsealed her box of silk-worm eggs. She spread them out on a table to hatch. Then she sat down on the floor by the table and consulted her pamphlet. Sandy settled himself on the floor beside her. Martitia alternately read the book and talked to the dog.

"It says, Sandy, that the silkworm eggs will hatch into worms in twenty-four hours or thirty-six hours. Then I must have tender, new mulberry leaves to begin feeding the worms with. I had best start picking the leaves today and put them in a covered basket in the corner of the barn where it's cool and dry. Then I'll have a supply ready on hand. The worms must be fed with fresh leaves three times a day. And I must never pick the leaves and feed them to the worms while there is rain or dew upon the leaves. That will make the worms sick. They might die. I'd best keep a supply in the barn for two days in advance, so if it rains, I'll not be lacking for leaves."

Martitia went out with her basket to the mulberry orchard near by. She picked the tenderest, youngest leaves. Sandy accompanied her.

Next day Martitia turned pale with excitement when she found that the infinitesimal eggs of dull brown had hatched into vast numbers of threadlike worms. She laid over the worms young mulberry leaves and watched the worms attach themselves. Then with the mulberry stems she lifted up the leaves and the attached worms. She spread them out on her tables as she desired.

"I've started, Sandy. Just look at my precious worms that are going to spin silk to send Jonathan to Judge Debow's in June!" Martitia's eyes glowed. Sandy looked up and barked.

"Were you reminding me, Sandy, how I must keep the tables cleared of the worms' litter? And were you reminding me of the thousand pounds of leaves I've got to tote in the next four weeks? Ruth says I can't do it. But I can, Sandy. See if I can't. I can do anything I set my mind to."

Martitia found the first stage of the worms easy enough to handle. The insects were small and could eat little during the first four days. She spread out her tender mulberry leaves thin. She had to clear the litter only once. It was simple to scatter fresh leaves in one corner of her tables, let the worms attach themselves to the leaves, lift up the leaves to a clean place, then sweep the old litter away with a small broom. By repeating the process her tables were soon clean. She went about the mulberry orchard and the barn singing as she worked. It took only four or five pounds of leaves, she estimated, to satisfy her worms during the first stage.

"Who says I can't raise silkworms all by myself?" she asked Sandy.

Sandy whimpered.

"You're not warning me what comes next when the worms get larger, are you, Sandy?"

On the fifth day the worms changed their skins and seemed to get hungrier. In this second stage Martitia had to move about with a livelier step to keep the tables cleared of litter and to provide fresh new leaves. In three days she reckoned that she had to tote fifteen pounds of leaves from the orchard to the barn. She began to look more preoccupied.

The worms changed their skins again on the eighth day. Martitia grew alarmed at the appetite of the rapidly enlarging creatures. They seemed never to have enough leaves to satisfy them. The larger leaves did for them now. Martitia set the ladder against the taller trees in the orchard. Back and forth, back and forth, she trudged with her wagon and basket to the barn. She reckoned this time that the worms ate all of forty or fifty pounds of leaves from the eighth to the fourteenth day.

On the fourteenth day the worms acquired new skins yet a third time. By now the creatures had got quite sizable.

Ruth came down to the hay barn to inspect Martitia's charges. "They look very large and healthy, Martitia," she conceded grudgingly. "But your little book says that in the fourth stage, which comes next, you've got to feed the worms one hundred and twenty-five pounds of leaves. You'll give out long before the twenty-second day ends that fourth stage. Think of all the litter they'll make. And suppose it rains for a week. You'll have to admit soon that you're defeated. You'll get tired of toting leaves and cleaning litter. You'll give up and let the worms die."

"I won't," said Martitia loudly.

"Yes, you will. Even if you contrive to keep going through the fourth stage you'll give up when the last ten days come. Your pamphlet says that the worms eat *seven hundred and sixty-four pounds* of leaves in the last ten days before spinning their cocoons. You can't tote seven hundred and sixty-four pounds of leaves. Nor can you clean up the litter. I look to see you admit defeat and let them die in desperation, even with Addison to give you some help."

Martitia thinned her lips. "It seems to me, Ruth, that you spend all your time studying my pamphlet book. I'll never give up. I'd rather die trying."

Ruth went away. The Virginia girl stared mutinously after her. Back to the mulberry orchard trudged Martitia with her wagon and basket. Wearily she placed the ladder against a tree and set to work picking more leaves. Wearily she changed and swept the tables and boards.

On the twenty-second day the worms adjusted their final coats. Martitia cast a despairing look at the voracious, enlarged insects. She toted leaves endlessly.

On the twenty-third afternoon Addison appeared from the fields early. He roared into the hay barn and watched Martitia feed her never-satisfied charges. "Dwarf," said Addison, "let's just bake a batch of half-moon apple pies and feed the worms all at once and kill them off. 'Tisn't decent for any living creatures to eat so much."

Martitia leaned her head against the wall of the hay barn. Addison patted her shoulder. "Don't despair, Dwarf. I'm your man from now on every afternoon. Just wait and see how fast I can tote leaves."

Martitia resumed work. When she glanced up from one of the tables later she saw the wagon with the basket of leaves appear in the door drawn by a queer object. The object had leaves stuffed behind its ears. The object jumped and snorted, presenting a pair of large ears to Martitia to scratch.

"Oh, Addison! Playing pony to take my mind off these great hungry worms! You deserve a gold medal for reward."

Addison crawled about the barn floor, snorting and sniffing the air, bumping the wagon so that leaves flew in every direction. Martitia laughed helplessly. Addison wiggled his ears.

"Will you teach me to wiggle my ears, Addison?"

"Yes."

On the twenty-eighth afternoon it began to grow strangely dark and cloudy. An ominous hush hung over the mulberry orchard and the barn. Only two days' supply of dry leaves was accumulated in the hay barn.

Addison faced Martitia with dismay written on his face. "If it sets in to rain for three or four days we're lost, Dwarf. The leaves will be sopping wet. We need two more days' supply to keep us going."

Ruth appeared in the doorway. "I've just come from studying the almanac, Martitia. The almanac says we're going to have rainy weather till July. You might as well give up this business before straining further."

Martitia looked at her. "Take that basket yonder, Ruth, this very minute. Get out yonder in the mulberry orchard and start picking leaves. With you to help, Addison and I can get enough leaves by dark to keep us going. If it starts raining we'll keep on picking in the rain. I can spread the wet leaves out tonight on the floor and dry them in two days. Get going in a hurry."

"Every tub ought to stand on its own bottom. I didn't offer to help."

"I don't care whether you offered to help or not. I'm standing on my own bottom. But I'll stand on *your* bottom, too, if need be to send Jonathan to Orange County." Martitia faced the other girl fiercely.

Ruth looked astounded beyond speech. She strode obediently out to the mulberry orchard.

Dusk came, bringing with it showers of rain. Three figures still worked madly under the mulberry trees. Before the great rain squall broke over the grove Addison, Martitia, and Ruth ran wildly into the hay barn. There they stood, watching the downpour outside, and surveyed the great mounds of green mulberry leaves heaped up in the dry hay barn.

Ruth looked from the mulberry leaves to Martitia. Unmistakable admiration showed in her pronounced features. "I never took orders from anyone else in my life before except Pa and Ma. I've got respect for you, Martitia. Let's be friends."

Martitia saw how the long battle between her and Ruth was over. She reached out a small hand and grasped Ruth's large one. "Thank you for helping. I'll never forget it. If we live to be a hundred years old we'll be friends."

Addison turned a somersault over one of the mounds of mulberry leaves. Outside the rain roared and whipped through the drenched trees. The two girls stood hand in hand, watching the rain through the barn door. Behind them, on the tables and planks, the silkworms kept on eating.

Four days later Martitia's great worms stopped eating. Green, nearly transparent, they climbed the bent branches of oak with which the tables were arched into tents now.

They began spinning their silky oval cocoons. In a week they had all finished their cycle of life. Out of the eggs and the mulberry leaves, in the space of six weeks, had come rich and durable silk.

Martitia took down the bent branches, pulled off the innumerable cocoons, cleared them of loose tow, and set them in baskets for their final finishing. Lest the living moths inside the spun cocoons eat their way out and break the miles of silk thread wrapped about them, she had to stifle the chrysalides within. This she did by setting the cocoons in pans and tins in the big Dutch oven, moderately heated, for half an hour. Her work was at last finished. She surveyed the baskets of silky cocoons in weary, triumphant joy.

On the last day of May, Dr. David let Addison drive Martitia with her cocoons over in the wagon to Jamestown. Ruth went along. The three young people talked and sang as they drove. Even Ruth smiled a little at last. From sunup to sundown they used in making the trip.

Madame de la Brousse took Martitia into her arms when she caught sight of her on the steps of the house in the Mulberry Grove. She kissed both her cheeks. She praised the size and quality of Martitia's cocoons. She weighed the cocoons and pronounced them to total a hundred and four pounds.

Martitia went away carrying fifty-two dollars in currency in her pocket. But she could not leave until she and Addison and Ruth had eaten dinner at Madame de la Brousse's elegant French table. And Madame was not content till Martitia had played the spinet in the parlor.

"Come again, child," she said in parting. "You only in this part of the County of Guilford seem to speak my language well. Your words talk to my heart as well as to my ears. When you marry that young man with the firm mouth who came to call on me with you and your cousin Sarah last summer I shall send you the blue silk dress to wear in your trousseau."

Martitia answered earnestly: "You must send the silk dress then to my cousin Sarah if you wish it worn for that young man with the firm mouth whom you mention."

Madame only smiled and shook her head.

That night Martitia handed the fifty-two dollars in currency into Dr. David's keeping. "When Jonathan comes next week please don't tell him, sir, who made the money. He mightn't wish to take it and use it. You yourself said he was proud."

"Perhaps you're right, child. No one will say a word of this silk culture of yours to Jonathan. Jonathan is proud. We will keep Quaker silence on the work of those two small hands of yours. With the little I can add Jonathan can go to Judge Debow's. He can stay in Orange County till I get on my feet with a decent grain crop this fall. You're a smart child, Martitia."

CHAPTER XXII

She Learned to Laugh

ON THE MORNING of her eighteenth birthday, June fourth, Martitia sat at the loom in the spring-house attic weaving blue jean. Jonathan sat in a near-by chair and watched her. Over their heads the red-pepper strings swung lightly in a warm wind through the window.

"Last night when I got home you seemed far away and strange, Martitia. So like a young lady instead of a little girl you've grown since last September when I left home. I was a little afraid of you there on the porch with the others. But today you seem more like the small Martitia that got out of Pa's gig two years ago in front of the Gardner house."

Martitia answered in a wistful voice: "In two weeks you'll go away to Judge Debow's, not to come back at all. At least you'll only come back for visits to your pa and ma. You'll be a famous lawyer soon and go to the Legislature."

"And does it make you sad to have me become a lawyer and go to Raleigh to the Legislature? Last summer you worked to help me overcome my diffidence at speech-making. I should tell you, Martitia, that after my speech-making to you in the mulberry grove last year I contrived to gain a medal for speech-making at Mr. Bingham's school this spring."

Martitia stopped weaving. Her face grew bright. "I knew you could learn to make speeches to strangers. 'Twas only a little practice you needed. You could win anything in the world you chose if you set yourself to try for it."

The young man did not answer for a while. He turned his head away and stared out the window. When he spoke finally, his words seemed to bear no connection with what he had been saying before. His eyes were stern.

"It was a grave home-coming when I rode up to the porch last night in the dusk. Only Addison and Pa and Milton were there of the Gardner men to greet me. I was glad that Milton had come over visiting from Asheborough to welcome me. But I minded me how there should have been six of us Gardner men: Pa and the five brothers we've always been before."

Martitia stared at her hands. Jonathan went on after a pause: "What happened last November came nigh to breaking us Gardner brothers. Milton and Barzillai and Addison and I have written each other letters about that. Pa and Ma look older. I reckon that your own heart has come near to breaking, too, Martitia."

Martitia could not answer. She bowed her dark head.

Jonathan went on questioningly: "They say that time

makes folks forget even the worst of things, Martitia. I wonder about the truth of that. I reckon I'll be wondering about the truth of that for many months to come."

He got up suddenly, as though the attic room were not large enough to hold his spare, tall body. He peered restlessly out the window. "Come on. Quit your weaving of new pants for Addison. 'Tisn't sensible to lurk in attics when there's sunshine outdoors."

Martitia followed Jonathan out into the sun.

On the third day of Jonathan's visit Martitia sat on the front porch of Dr. David's house in the early-afternoon sunlight. She wore a neatly mended and beautifully laundered white muslin dress. The blue ribbon about her hair was trimly tied. Above her a blackbird was singing. Martitia sat alone and listened to the blackbird sing. She felt her mouth curve into a smile. The smile held humor as well as sweetness.

The dreamy quiet of the yard was broken by a salvo of loud voices, the clatter of horses' hoofs, and the barking of dogs. Martitia stirred on the stone steps and leaned forward. Those Gardner boys were home again from heaven-knew-where! They came galloping into the yard: Jonathan, Milton, and Addison, on horseback. Dogs leaped at the horses' heels.

Martitia left the steps and went across the grass to meet them. Addison and Milton got down from their horses in a jumble of big shoes and tousled heads and blue jeans. Jonathan kept to his saddle. His hazel eyes gleamed down at Martitia below him.

He rode his horse forward toward her. Martitia drew backward on the grass. Jonathan prodded his mare a few more steps toward the girl. She withdrew slightly, still moving backward on the grass toward the house. Jonathan prodded his mare again. Martitia took one good look upward at the mischief lurking in his eyes.

She turned and fled toward the porch to escape the horse and rider now openly pursuing her from behind. When she reached the top of the four stone steps she turned and looked triumphantly at Jonathan on his horse.

"Now you can't get me!" she taunted joyfully. Her laughter rang out through the yard. She gloried noisily in her speed at outwitting and eluding her pursuer.

Jonathan's face glowed. "You've truly learned to laugh, Martitia."

Martitia wiggled her ears at him.

Without warning Jonathan spurred his horse. The girl's laughter turned into a wild scream. Jonathan's mare plunged and reared up the steps. Martitia fled shrieking into the hip-roofed house. Jonathan pursued her across the porch on horseback, his horse's hoofs clattering and rumbling on the sturdy boards.

CHAPTER XXIII

In the Icehouse

JONATHAN SURVEYED his father at breakfast next morning. "Pa, I was down at the mulberry grove early this morning. It looks like a strange blight has struck the mulberry trees. All the leaves have vanished from the lower branches. What do you reckon is the matter?"

Addison choked on his breakfast. Martitia grew crimson.

Dr. David answered calmly: "Son, there's many blights that strike trees. The caterpillars have spoiled some of the elms' branches. Blights seem to be nature's business, not man's."

Martitia breathed a sigh of relief. Addison appeared scarcely able to contain his exuberance at Jonathan's question and Martitia's plight. His mother looked at him in quiet reproof.

Jonathan continued: "I'm going to the fields with you today, Pa, and put in some work on the crops."

Dr. David answered: "I'd be glad of your help." He

grinned at Milton. "Doctor Milton would be a likely physician for a hoe today too."

Milton pretended to sigh gustily. "All right, Pa. I may be a doctor now and a visitor, but I reckon I still know how to nurse a hoe."

Ruth entered the conversation around the breakfast table. She addressed her mother. "Mary Macy reckoned yesterday when I saw her that her ma was going to begin preserving green relishes this morning. She had a mind to ask how you preserve the cucumbers in vinegar."

Eunice looked at Ruth. "Thee and I might show a neighborly spirit today by walking over to the Macys' and lending a hand with the relish-making. We could be back by midday. Martitia can cook the dinner. Eh, Martitia?"

Martitia spoke quickly: "I'd like it uncommon well, Aunt Eunice, to cook the dinner today. Milton and Jonathan should know how fine are the half-moon apple pies I can fashion. And I'll mix up one of my spoon breads."

Jonathan surveyed his mother solemnly. "It's likely, Ma, that all of us will get poisoned from eating the food if Martitia cooks it by herself. You recollect how ill all of us boys got after eating the first batch of bread that Martitia baked for the Gardners."

Martitia twinkled. "My cooking is good enough to set before Mr. Henry Clay himself."

Jonathan burst out laughing. "What do you know about Mr. Henry Clay?"

"A great deal. I've been reading Doctor David's weekly paper from Greensborough. And I've been studying the books you left at home. I'm a very learned female, Jonathan." Martitia's eyes gleamed.

Jonathan inspected her in alarm. "Don't turn into an

intellectual female, Martitia. You'll never get you a husband if you do. Menfolks want to know more about everything than their womenfolks do."

Martitia fell into a brown study. Presently she spoke again: "Are you going over to Jamestown before you travel back to Orange County, Jonathan?"

Jonathan looked startled. "Why, no. I've nothing to go to Jamestown for."

Martitia dropped her eyes. A small smile hovered about the corners of her lips. "I only asked."

Dr. David and the three boys left for the fields. After a while Eunice and Ruth prepared to set forth too.

"We will go now to the Macys', Martitia," said Eunice in departing. "Thee must fetch the mutton roast from the icehouse when thee is ready for putting it in the oven. I cut off a roast yesterday and set it handy to be got out when needed. Thee will not even need the lantern to look by. Here is the key to the icehouse."

Martitia hesitated. Then she took the key and watched Eunice and Ruth disappear up the road. She held the key gingerly. The one thing at the Gardner house that Martitia feared, she reckoned, was that key to the icehouse and what it represented.

She confided her fear now to Sandy, who came up the back steps and followed her about the kitchen. "I love to cook apple pies and bread and vegetables and dumplings, Sandy. I love to make butter and to weave cloth. I even like to clean house and iron clothes. But I'm afeared to go down into the deep dark, cold icehouse. I reckon it's because the place is so cold and dark 'way down there in the pit in the middle of the earth."

Sandy wagged his tail. Martitia went upstairs and put

on her best blue hair ribbon. She decided to leave her weaving till afternoon. She must prepare a more savory, more varied dinner than even Sarah Gardner Mendenhall could prepare!

"Menfolks may like lively conversation, Sandy, and ribbons. But they also like dumplings and good meat and relishes. I don't know which they prefer most. I'll take no chances."

Martitia set about her preparations. After a while she took the icehouse key and set forth sadly with Sandy to fetch the mutton roast from its cold abiding place in the ground under the peaked roof. She carried a basket over her arm.

She talked to Sandy all the way across the back yard under the poplar trees. "Only because I know 'tis my duty, Sandy, do I ever go into that dreadful dark place yonder. I'm afeared of the icehouse. My other fears I've conquered by patterning myself after the Gardners. But this one fear I've never got over. I should be ashamed of myself. You recollect, Sandy, how even the Gardners' Spanish sheep dog was not afeared of a wolf. I ought to be as fearless in my own trust-keeping as the Gardners' Spanish sheep dog was in tending his sheep. A trust is a trust. However small my trust may seem to anyone else, it seems large to me. Only because Aunt Eunice makes it my duty to go down into the icehouse do I ever go. And today I've got a trust to keep. So I'll keep it."

Martitia reached the icehouse. Over the pit the shingle roof reached from the ground on each side to the comb. Martitia looked fearfully at the great door in the ground beneath, opening outward almost on the level with the earth.

"I'm afeared of it, Sandy. But I'll put the key in the lock and open that door upward. I'll prop it against the post that's set there to hold it steady while I climb inside and go down the ladder. Think of all that steep ladder of rungs downward, fifteen feet of it, Sandy! And think how dark it is down there with only the light from the open door above to show me how to find the roast of mutton that Aunt Eunice cut off yesterday. Oh, Sandy, I don't *want* to go down there into that icy-cold pit in the ground with all those ice blocks piled about me! But I'm going. I'll get the roast and put it in the basket over my arm while I climb back upward."

Martitia unlocked the door in the ground and lifted it up with a great effort of muscles. She propped it against the waiting post. An icy breath of air came up to her from the opening.

"Stay here, Sandy, and bark to me while I'm getting the roast. I'll shut my eyes while I take the first steps down the ladder. Then maybe it won't seem so dreadful."

Martitia started down the ladder, her eyes tightly shut. Suddenly, whether from a farewell leap of Sandy's or from the caught edge of her wide skirts or her sleeve, the door of the icehouse tottered and fell shut upon her. Martitia felt herself knocked from the ladder into infinite blackness and coldness and oblivion. One moment she was safe in the sunshiny world. Next moment she was nowhere.

She had no idea how long she must have lain there on the sawdust floor of the icehouse before she came to herself again. Her head ached. A stabbing pain struck through her right leg when she tried to move. Around her was the mystery of wintertime. The icehouse was black and frozen and silent. The only sound in her ears was a faint scratching noise from the shut door fifteen feet above her. Faithful Sandy sought to reach his mistress, she reckoned! She lay on the sawdust, numb and terrified.

I shall lie here alone for hours and die. No one is at the house to miss me or know I am gone. By the time Jonathan comes back from the fields I shall be frozen to death. I shall never see the sunshine again or look upon Jonathan's face.

With desperate determination Martitia tried to move herself. She must have lost consciousness at the pain, she reckoned. When she found herself thinking again the scratching sound above her head had died away.

You've left me, too, Sandy. Clarkson told you never to forsake me.

In her gathering numbness of pain and absolute cold Martitia could no longer connect her thoughts.

Was this the way you felt, Clarkson, when you came to die, off there in Wilmington? Were you forsaken by every living creature? You died to save other people's lives. I shall only die to obey Aunt Eunice's command to come to the icehouse. It's such a little thing to die for. Yet I tried to keep my trust, too, Clarkson. Won't you come and hold my hand till I can't think any more?

Martitia lay still. Then in the blackness she saw dimly a light far above her. Infinitely far away she heard voices. Someone lifted her up. She cried out with the pain. But she spoke in agonized relief.

"You *did* come to find me, Clarkson!"

Like words spoken in a dream she heard a voice that sounded like Jonathan's say: "Pa, reach your hands down as far as you can to take Martitia. I've got her in my arms now."

Then for a while she neither heard nor thought any more.

When she began to know what was happening again she figured it must be late afternoon. The light across her face was dim. She lay in her own bed under the eaves, with blankets piled upon her. Her head ached. Her right leg felt stiff as though in a vise. Dr. David sat by the bed.

As her eyes opened he spoke. "Thee is all right, Daughter. Don't thee try to talk. Sandy came to Jonathan in the bottom land. Sandy kept barking and leaping at Jonathan till my son knew something was wrong and called to me to come with him and to follow Sandy. Sandy led us to the icehouse. Jonathan found thee and brought thee up. Thy right leg is broken. Thee had a bad blow on thy skull too. But thee is too young and lissome to have been injured otherwise. I'll take care of thee."

Martitia felt weak tears slide down her cheeks. Her lips seemed too tired to form words. She shut her lids. When she woke again it was dark. A candle burned on the bureau. Dr. David bent over her with something in a cup.

"Take this, Daughter."

She took it spoonful by spoonful. It burned. "My head aches dreadfully, sir."

"It will be better by morning."

Waking or fitfully sleeping, it seemed to Martitia that Dr. David was always there. His hand on her wrist felt steady and warm. His ear, when he put it now and then to her chest, comforted her in the loneliness of her withdrawal from ordinary life. She slept when she could. Finally she knew by the light through the window that it must be dawn. She fell into a sound sleep.

Eunice was by her when she roused. Familiar and natural looked the world. Martitia spoke strongly.

"What o'clock is it, ma'am?"

"It's four o'clock in the afternoon. Thee has slept since dawn. David says the danger of thy contracting lung fever is past. He examined thy chest before he went away a half hour ago to steal a little sleep. He has sat with thee since yesterday noon. Hardly would he take a turn on the porch for three minutes, leaving Milton or me to spell him in thy room. David loves thee, child. All the Gardners are fond of thee. Thee gave us a bad scare."

Martitia said hungrily: "May I have something to eat, ma'am?"

Eunice's face softened. "Hunger is a good sign. Thee has borne well the blow upon thy skull, David says."

"My head doesn't ache so. But for my stiff leg, I should get up."

"The stiffness in thy leg is from the splint David has put upon it. Thee has no inside injury. 'Twas the fever in the lungs David feared from thy long exposure to cold. Thy chest is clear, though. Thee can have whatever thee wishes to eat."

"I don't wish any mutton roast, ma'am," said Martitia with a wry face.

"I'll bring thee milk and chicken soup. Ruth will sit with thee while I am gone."

"Has Jonathan come back from the fields, ma'am?"

"My son Jonathan has never gone to the fields. He sat in the kitchen all night and all day pestering his father for news of thee."

Martitia said nothing.

It was a week before Dr. David carried her downstairs. He deposited her in Grandfather Daniel's chair by the kitchen window. Ruth ran to fetch a straight-backed chair to prop up Martitia's stiff leg. Addison and Milton and Jonathan gathered about her.

"Dwarf," said Addison, "you gave us a dreadful scare. We can't get along without our undersized, malicious midget." He kissed the top of Martitia's head.

Milton tweaked her ear. "At any rate I've learned some fine points of doctoring from observing Pa's masterly treatment of your broken leg and battered noodle. I've had as much medical training as Pa or any other doctor. But Pa still knows more than I do."

Jonathan said nothing. He only stood looking at Martitia. His expression baffled the girl. It was withdrawn.

Milton went blithely on: "Jonathan's visit is over. He and I will set off together at dawn tomorrow. Only he'll go northeast and I'll go south."

Martitia looked swiftly at Jonathan. "Are you truly going away tomorrow?"

"Yes, Judge Debow expects me soon. There's nothing more for me to do here."

"You'll not come back for a year?"

"Likely not, Martitia."

Martitia grew silent. She listened wistfully to the other Gardners laughing around her. Jonathan was silent too.

His last words to the girl before Dr. David carried her back upstairs that evening were a formal good-by.

"Pa won't have brought you down by dawn, when Milton and I leave tomorrow. I wish to say good-by to you."

"Good-by, Jonathan." Martitia searched his face.

Jonathan looked down at Sandy, who crouched by the girl's chair. "Sandy may have saved your life, Martitia. Clarkson would be glad of that if he could know it."

※ ※ ※ ※ ※ ※ ※ ※ ※ ※ ※ ※ ※ ※ ※

CHAPTER XXIV

Umbrella of Fire

WARM WINDS BLEW over the grain fields at
Centre. Rains came at intervals. The sun shone
magnificently. Summer turned the fields green then gold.
September brought the ending to the finest harvest in five
years for Guilford County.

Martitia's broken leg was long since mended. She
drove with Dr. David in his gig to the grist mill one day
in early fall. Dr. David spoke in triumph.

"The crops have outdone themselves this summer.
I've currency enough in sight for Jonathan to continue at
Judge Debow's till spring. He'll be ready for his licensing
by June, Jonathan will. This is a merry autumn for the
Gardners."

Martitia gave him a shining look.

"Without your aid in tiding Jonathan over this summer he'd be another season getting through his law work.
Whenever Jonathan comes home in the spring I aim to
tell him the truth about your work in the hay barn last

May. His pride can't stand in the way of his accepting what's already past. Jonathan should know about your service."

"He will only hate me, sir, if you make him feel beholden to me in any way. Please don't tell Jonathan."

Dr. David turned in the gig. "Do you truly think that my son Jonathan could ever hate you?"

Martitia answered painfully: "If he does not already somewhat hate me, why should he have gone away with no words to me in June save the cool words of a stranger?"

Dr. David hesitated. He drew a long breath. "I see there's a matter that needs clearing up in your memory. Do you recall anything of your thoughts or words on the day that you fell to the bottom of the icehouse?"

Martitia lifted her head quickly. "Not much, sir. Not very clearly. I was full of strange fancies. I couldn't connect my thoughts. The world seemed very far away."

"I reckoned as much after that blow on your skull. Do you remember anyone who was in your thoughts that day?"

Martitia frowned. "I seem to recollect, sir, now that you cudgel my brain, that when I thought myself dying I fancied Clarkson had come to be with me."

"Do you recall the moment when my son Jonathan lifted you up from the icehouse floor?"

"Not very well, sir."

"You don't recall speaking to him?"

"No sir."

"Well, in that moment you called my son Jonathan by Clarkson's name."

Martitia stared whitely at Dr. David.

"I saw the look, child, on Jonathan's face when he

brought you up into the light. I knew what your speech had cost him. Those sons of mine love each other. Death does not alter their love or their unity. While Clarkson's name was still on your lips do you think that my son Jonathan could speak to you as aught save a stranger?"

Martitia bowed her head.

Dr. David went on slowly: "I think Jonathan loved you before ever Clarkson did, Martitia. That first day when I lifted you down from the gig in front of our house here at Centre, Jonathan's face showed a new heaven and a new earth."

Martitia looked up swiftly. "He had a strange way of telling it, sir."

"Jonathan could never show his heart openly as others might. And when he came back from Hillsborough that first spring he found, as we all knew, that Clarkson had set his whole heart upon you. He could as soon have cut his own jugular vein as to have stood between Clarkson and the woman he cared for. Those brothers stand united."

Martitia could find no speech to answer with.

Dr. David spoke his next sentences as though they came with great difficulty. "When my son Clarkson died I cannot be sure how Jonathan felt about you. It's likely he thought he had no right to come between Clarkson's memory and your loving heart till you turned to him of your own free will, if ever you did."

Martitia broke out breathlessly: "But, sir, 'twas always Jonathan I loved."

"I know that, child. Jonathan doesn't know it, though. Perhaps he felt in June that when you laughed with him you were turning toward him at last. But in the icehouse you called on Clarkson's name. A person who thinks himself dying is likely to call on the name of the one he truly loves."

"But I didn't know what I spoke, sir. 'Twas only that Clarkson had been called on to die also. I thought in my muddled head he might somehow come to help me die as well."

"My son Jonathan couldn't know that."

"Why didn't you tell him, sir?" Martitia spoke desolately.

"Jonathan isn't a man anyone can approach on matters within himself. He stands alone."

"Then Jonathan will never understand."

"Perhaps his sternness will yield to some strong happening from outside his life. My son Jonathan is a little hard, but he is only human."

Dr. David turned his attention to the few yellow leaves appearing in the trees bordering the road to the mill. "Look at autumn. Rejoice at our Gardner prosperity. The Lord meant us to be glad, not to be sorrowful."

Martitia surveyed the yellow leaves and managed a smile.

She remembered to rejoice all through September at the splendid appearance of the world during that beautiful autumn of 1833. September pushed hard on October. The nuts were the finest in years. And like the rain of nuts from the walnuts and hickories, the days of October seemed richer than in any man's memory before. All creation seemed to hold its breath before the spectacle of such abundant yield. November broke in a cool crest over Centre.

Martitia went to the front door of the Gardners' house in answer to a knock on the late afternoon of November 13,

1833. Dusk had darkened the porch. She peered into the dimness and saw a man's tall figure standing there. A hoarse voice spoke from the shadows.

"I am a poor stranger, and I need lodging for the night. May I secure food and shelter, ma'am?"

Remembering how Dr. David and Addison and even Ruth had not come up from the barn and how she and Eunice were alone in the house, Martitia felt herself shiver at the strange, hoarse voice in the shadows. For a minute she could not answer.

The hoarse voice insisted again from the dimness: "Ma'am, you wouldn't refuse a bite to eat and a cot to sleep on to a poor devil who's hungry and cold, would you? I've heard tell the folks in this house were good Christian Quakers."

Martitia summoned a sturdy voice. "Sir, I'll go call my aunt. She's the lady of the house. She will speak with you. Tarry here a minute."

Martitia retired abruptly into the kitchen where Eunice was completing supper. "Aunt Eunice, there's a dreadful, hoarse-voiced stranger man upon the porch who asks shelter for the night. What shall I do about him? Must I ask him in to share our supper and to sleep in the spare bedroom this night? He sounds as if he were a dangerous tramp who might steal the Gardners' pewter spoons and mugs. He has a fierce voice."

Eunice looked at Martitia. She went to a corner and secured a riding whip of Dr. David's. "If the stranger be an honest poor fellow, then I will bid him share the Gardners' hospitality. If he be a rogue, then I will chastise him roundly with this whip."

Sturdily Eunice advanced to the door on to the front

porch, the whip held behind her. Martitia accompanied her valiantly. From the candlelit kitchen Eunice spoke into the shadowy porch:

"Friend, come into the light where I may speak with thee. I cannot bid thee welcome when thee is well-nigh unseen to me."

The man on the porch bunched his shoulders higher and drew the shadowy outline of his hat further over his face. "I'm a poor fellow, ma'am; I don't wish you to send me packing because of witnessing my rags. I'm honest but uncommon hungry. I could do with a bit of the fine supper whose smell floats to me here in the cold dark."

"Then come into the light where I may see thee."

"Is it frying apples that I smell with my poor nose, ma'am?"

"Not frying apples. 'Tis hot apple pies that my adopted daughter is cooking in the oven in the fireplace."

"If 'tis hot apple pies that I smell, ma'am, then I will come in with no further ado. Stand aside and let me pass."

Roughly the fellow upon the porch strode into the light and attempted to brush the small Quaker woman aside. Eunice lifted her whip. The candlelight from the kitchen lighted the stranger's face. The whip fell.

"My son Jonathan!"

Jonathan impishly dropped his hat upon the floor and lifted his mother clear off her feet. "Ma'am, can you contrive to give a welcome to a hungry tramp who has ridden on a horse all the way from Greensborough since three of the clock this afternoon?"

Eunice clung to him for a moment. He let her down to the floor once more. With a quick motion Eunice

lifted the whip and wrapped it smartly about Jonathan's
long legs.

"Though thee be my son, thee deserves a thrashing
for thy foolery in scaring thine own mother."

Jonathan broke into a delighted roar of laughter. Martitia stared at him with shining eyes. Jonathan took the
whip from his mother's hand.

"Now, Ma, don't let Martitia see what a temper you
have. I'll wager Martitia has never seen you angry before.
Martitia should know how hot-tempered was little Eunice
Gardner when first Pa got you and took you in hand."

Eunice spoke with vigor: "Come into the house, Son,
and eat thy supper. Martitia must have felt it in her bones
that thee was coming. She has fashioned half-moon apple pies as an uncommon treat for the Gardners' supper.
Thy father and thy brother will lift up the roof when
they come in from the barn and find thee here among us.
What has brought thee all the way from Orange County
and Judge Debow?"

"Judge Debow himself is no longer in Orange County,
but in the county seat of Guilford. He came to hold
court at Greensborough. He figured I could travel with
him and gain experience at watching the processes of the
law. He also figured that I might wish to ride over on
horseback and visit with my hot-tempered little ma in
the Gardner house at Centre. So here I be, Ma. And here
I shall stay till the morrow's noon. At that hour I must
return to Greensborough and rejoin Judge Debow."

Jonathan turned to Martitia. His hazel eyes measured
her. He was suddenly grave. "Have you a welcome for a
stranger, Martitia?"

Martitia answered softly: "Welcome, Jonathan."

Then Dr. David and Ruth and Addison came into the kitchen from the back porch and caught sight of Jonathan standing in the front door with Eunice and Martitia.

Such a turmoil of Gardner laughter Martitia had never heard before. The very house itself seemed to rock on its foundations. Addison and Dr. David and Jonathan roared and slapped each other's shoulders in jubilant triumph. All the time Eunice watched her eldest son's face. Martitia went about dishing up supper with Ruth's help.

At supper Jonathan turned teasing eyes upon Martitia at last. "So you've actually learned to make half-moon apple pies, Martitia?" He nibbled an edge of one crisp little pie. "It tastes right good." He nibbled another mouthful and addressed his father. "Pa, what is it in the Bible about the little book that tasted sweet to the tongue but was bitter to the belly? Do you reckon, Pa, that there's any connection between Martitia's pies and the Bible story? Had I better eat the pies or not?"

Dr. David thumped one great hand on the table joyfully. "Eat the pies, Son. Martitia is a better cook even than your ma is now." He twinkled across the table wickedly at Eunice.

Eunice threw him her grave, indulgent smile.

It seemed to Martitia that never before had an evening flown so fast as this one flew. Listening to Jonathan talk about Judge Debow's house and his law work made every minute enchanting to Martitia. She looked desolate when Dr. David pointed to the clock and said:

"It's all of half after nine o'clock. We must go to our beds. The lateness of the hour is a tribute to Jonathan's skill in speech-making." He turned to his eldest son.

"Son, sit with me a while longer. There is a matter on which I wish to talk to you alone."

Martitia went away with the others. She held her candle high and climbed the steps to her room. Below her she could hear the murmur of two deep voices. Their rumbling whisper followed her all the way up to the dormered room under the eaves.

She went over to the window and sat down in her chair. Through the panes she could see the serene stars staring down at her from the dark sky, as they had stared down upon her that first night of her stay at Centre. She pondered the stars and Jonathan's face.

Jonathan is under the same roof with me. Though he never speaks to me as aught save a friendly stranger, I can watch his face and hear his voice for a little while.

Martitia rose and got a cape. She wrapped it about her and huddled there, watching the steady stars, unwilling to sleep while Jonathan still talked to Dr. David downstairs.

Then suddenly Martitia stopped breathing. An umbrella of fire opened out in the heavens and covered the whole sky! A great rain of fire streaked and ribbed the sky with unearthly light! Stars rocked and whirled in their courses, falling and colliding and bursting into flames. Like snowflakes in a winter tempest, the stars fell by the thousands. They streamed in great banners across the dark. The whole air seemed full of them.

Martitia jumped up screaming. Screaming, she ran to the door and fled down the steps, crying as she ran: "This is the end of the world! This is the Judgment Day! The stars are all falling down! The stars are all falling down!"

Bone-white and shaking, she burst into the kitchen.

One look at her face and Dr. David and Jonathan were on their feet.

"Look out at the heavens! The stars are all falling out of the sky! The end of the world has come!"

Jonathan and Dr. David turned swiftly toward the front porch. Jonathan jerked open the door. Martitia followed. The three of them ran out into the yard before the house. There was no need for the girl to point. The whole sky was full of that terrible, starry rain. Colliding and whirling, the stars ribbed the sky with their fiery streaks. With bright, long trains they traversed the heavens, shining red and white and yellow. They gleamed and darted by the thousands. No sound came from any of them.

Dr. David gasped: "Never did rain fall thicker than these stars are falling. East, west, north, and south, it is all the same. God save the world and us sinners upon it!"

Jonathan spoke in a strong, hushed voice: "This is the most marvelous spectacle the heavens have ever caused the eyes of men to witness."

Martitia reached out her hand and put it into Jonathan's. "Is it the end of the world? Is it the Judgment Day, Jonathan?"

Jonathan drew her hand close. "If this is the end of the world don't thee be afeared. I'll not let thee witness it alone."

Dr. David turned toward the porch. "I'll waken Eunice. Ruth and Addison must be wakened too. Whatever is coming we must be together." He strode swiftly toward the house.

Eunice came down the steps to meet him. She moved

quietly, lightly. Ruth and Addison followed after her hand in hand.

"Martitia's cry roused us. Through the windows we witnessed what God is speaking to His people in the heavens this night. Terrible is the majesty of the Lord. Yet His kindness endureth forever."

She held out something to Dr. David. "Here is thy greatcoat, David. The night is cold." She turned to Jonathan. "Son, take thy coat also. Thee must be warm while thee watches God's plan for His people work out in the heavens this night. Martitia, has thee worn thy heavy wrappings? Be thy hands warm?"

Martitia moved her fingers in Jonathan's hold. "My hands be warm, ma'am."

"While we watch the majesty and the glory of the Lord we must use common sense. 'Tis not putting our trust in God to stand here fearfully gaping at the heavens. Best that we sit ourselves down upon the porch steps while we wait for the Divine will to make itself manifest."

Indomitably the little woman herded her flock to the steps. She saw that they were settled warmly there. She sat by her big husband through the long night hours, in calm acceptance of miracle or disaster. As the stars reeled above their heads she spoke quietly:

"Oh, Jerusalem, Jerusalem, thou that killest the prophets and stonest them which are sent unto thee, how often would I have gathered thy children together, even as a hen gathereth her chickens under her wings, and ye would not."

After a while she murmured: "Thy kingdom doth endure from generation to generation."

And still the stars fought with each other and fell streaking through the sky over their heads.

Martitia sat on the steps with her hand held tightly in Jonathan's. He said nothing. But she knew that his thoughts encompassed her securely. She waited quietly for whatever might come.

Just before dawn the stars stopped falling. One minute the heavens were full of blue and alien showers. Then, next minute, the old familiar stars were in their accustomed, stationary places. Presently, after six hours of chaos, the sun rose calmly, in its old accustomed way, over the pines and poplars. The world had not come to an end! Its inhabitants were still alive!

Martitia felt stiff and sore. She was amazed to find that with the coming of light she began to grow hungry. She looked shyly at Jonathan and withdrew her hand.

Dr. David stirred on the steps with a long sigh: "We are still alive! But 'twill be recorded as long as men live on this earth what took place in the heavens last night, on this November 13, 1833."

Eunice stood up. "Let us kneel together with the children, David, and offer praise to the Lord for sparing the world yet another while."

They knelt on the steps in the early dawn.

Eunice rose briskly. "Come, Ruth. Come, Martitia. We must prepare food for the men's breakfast."

Martitia followed Eunice up the steps and into the house.

CHAPTER XXV

Someday, Jonathan

AFTER BREAKFAST Jonathan spoke to Martitia "Must you sleep now, Martitia?"

"No, Jonathan."

"Then come with me to the mulberry grove. I've something to talk to you about."

"All right. I'll come. Only wait while I brush my hair and put on a clean pinafore."

Jonathan waited. Presently he and Martitia set out for the mulberry grove by the hay barn. Dr. David patted Martitia's head as she left.

The two young people said nothing at first. The world looked beautiful and precious to Martitia today. Had not the whole earth nearly passed away during the night just gone? And was not Jonathan here by her side now? She spoke earnestly.

"What do you reckon caused the stars to fall last

night, Jonathan? And where do you suppose they went? 'Twas a marvelous and a dreadful sight."

"The firmament is a strange book, Martitia. Men may someday learn to read better the messages written there for them to decipher. But not yet and not now."

"You speak like a prophet in the Bible."

Jonathan smiled wryly. "Here we are at the entrance of the mulberry grove. I'm no prophet to speak parables. But I reckon I'd fare better this day if I did have the tongue of Isaiah or Jeremiah to speak for me."

Martitia giggled. "I can fancy you all dressed up in a long flowing robe like Jeremiah's, with a white turban wrapped around your head. Oh, Jonathan, wouldn't you look strange?"

Jonathan paused under one of the mulberry trees. "This is where we rehearsed speech-making. Our spider is long since gone, but not what I learned from you here." He hesitated and looked down at her awkwardly. "Pa told me last night how the mulberry trees got their blight last spring. I'm obliged to you for that. At first I was angry when Pa told me. I didn't want to feel beholden to you, Martitia."

Martitia flushed and looked down at the toes of her shoes. Jonathan went on slowly, his face showing painful red: "I couldn't feel right about it till the stars started falling and you poked your little cold fingers in mine when you thought the world was ending. I don't mind being beholden to you, Martitia, if you feel that I'm the one you'd turn to when the whole world ends."

Martitia looked straight up at him. "That's the way I feel, Jonathan. That's the way I've always felt."

Jonathan reached out and took Martitia's hand nearest to him. One by one he bent back and stroked the five small fingers. "It was thy little hands that always brought me back to thee. Will thee give me both of thy hands to keep always, Martitia?"

"Yes, Jonathan."

"Wherever I go in life, will thee go with me?"

Martitia stretched out her other small hand and put it softly on Jonathan's sleeve. She looked up at him unwaveringly. "Yes, Jonathan."

Between tears she heard herself drop for the first time into the soft Quaker speech of his mother. "There'll come a day when thee will take me to the Governor's mansion. Someday, Jonathan, thee will be Governor of North Carolina."

"If so it be, Martitia, thy little hands will be the reason why."

Jonathan bent down and kissed her.